I0623534

Behind

the

Glass

M. Van

Behind the Glass

M. Van

42Links Publishing
Visit: www.42Links.net

Cover design by 42Links Publishing
Edited by Book helpline

ISBN: 978-90-824472-7-9

Chapter One

Julie

"Why do you think you're here?" someone in the room asked.

Afraid to look up, I wanted to curl my body into a tight ball, but I couldn't. The chair I sat in prevented it. Strong arms had lifted me from my hiding spot inside the cast iron tub, dragged me down the hall, and forced me to sit in this chair. The light hanging from the ceiling was dim, but it didn't prevent my eyes from stinging or tearing up. I couldn't see who asked the question, but I recoiled at the sound of his low, deep voice.

"Why!"

The sudden menacing boom of the piercing voice made me jump. Fear clamped down on my throat, restraining my words, but I knew he wanted his answer, and I needed to comply if I didn't want to spend another night in this chair. Anything would be better than the chair. But I didn't know the answer to his question, except for what I thought he wanted me to believe. Perhaps it wasn't so much what he wanted me to believe, but more what I believed.

"Because…" I started to say in a quivering voice, "I deserve it."

Chapter two

Julie

When handed a piece of paper and forced to write down one's thoughts, what does one write? Would it be the petty thoughts that clutter your mind like, *Oh, that cloud has a funny shape*, or *Check out the billion specks of dust floating in a beam of sunlight?* Unless you close your eyes, thoughts tend to drift in a direction brought on by the experience of senses from the past, the present, or whatever life *could* be, the things we hear, feel, and see until someone takes them from you. Unable to resist the demand to lay your soul bare at the risk of losing more than just your life, only to be left with an empty sheet of paper and a pen, with nothing left to do than to put it onto a page—and I will. If only to create the illusion of sharing these brief respite's with *you*.

A day not unlike any other day during these past few months was about to come to an end. I could tell from the reflection in the windows of the old Victorian building beyond the parking lot across the street. The old building loomed over its neighboring buildings in the fading sunlight, its tall windows the thresholds to what I could imagine being wide-open spaces with old wooden floors and blistering fireplaces; the tilted roof covered in anthracite-colored tiles glistened in the fading sunlight as if an open invitation to a variety of birds to rest their wings.

To the right, another elaborate building boasted its presence in an attempt to outshine its neighbor but failed, standing next to the old Victorian. From my little window the two buildings seemed joined at the hips, built side by side, but I knew they weren't. I could tell from the cars passing through the narrow street between them, where they waited in turn for their counterparts to pass by before they could pursue their own journeys.

A few cars probably belonging to its residents stood parked in front of the Victorian, most of them shining and brand-new as they gleamed in the fading sunlight. The golden-red sheen reflected from one of the cars made it seem almost invisible against the red bricks lining the lot. Near the end of the lot, two naked trees stood along the street that passed by my window. Their leaves hadn't yet returned, but I knew they soon would.

A man crossed the street wearing a jacket, but a young woman passed on her bike, showing her bare arms. Sunglasses rested on the bridge of her nose, and her hair danced in the wind. Spring had set in, and it wouldn't be long before summer came around the corner.

A white car emerged from underneath my window and into my line of sight. It turned into the lot. I didn't even hear it, and I imagined it to be one of those environmentally friendly, battery-driven vehicles. It parked between the white lines, and two people stepped out.

A gray-haired man emerged on the driver's side. He stretched his legs and shifted his head from left to right as if he had just stepped out from a long, tedious drive or maybe just had a long day. Before he could make his way to the back of the car, the door on the other side swung open. It took a while, but then a broad figure heaved itself out of the seat. A hand gripped the doorframe, and the other swung around and landed on the roof of the car.

The arm had the size of two bound baseball bats, and I was amazed that the roof didn't buckle underneath its weight. The large woman stuck to the baseball bats looked as if she had double-sized every meal she had ever eaten in her life.

She shuffled from the door, slammed it shut, and turned to the gray-haired man. He had busied himself by removing several bags from the trunk and then shutting the lid. The woman didn't even pretend to want to help the man; she only shuffled in line behind him as they made their way to the old Victorian. They didn't look like people who cared about the environment, I thought as the woman's large ass shuffled from my view.

The words seemed to flow freely as long as I kept them aloof, but that wasn't the story he'd want to read. I wasn't sure if he wanted a confession or an accurate account. I could only hope that the words revealed by this pen held by my shaking hand would appease him as I recounted the events of the recent past.

My heart stopped as I heard the rattle of keys. My eyes still lingered on the sun's beautiful reflection, while my strained body searched for ways to suck air into my lungs. Metal scraped on metal until the key found its hole, and then there was a click. The door opened, accompanied by a long, high-pitched squeak. Two thuds followed the first squeak before a second, long, high-pitched squeak announced the door closing. Inside the house, another door opened and closed before the silence returned and I reminded myself to breathe.

My heart had rediscovered its purpose, pounding against my chest, my throat clenched, and I listened intently while my eyes remained locked on the old Victorian across the lot. I couldn't break from the slow-fading light, dreading the moment it would disappear and feared the appending darkness. I didn't know how much time had passed, but none of the tension in my body had faltered since I'd heard those keys.

After the reflecting light had long disappeared from the tall windows, I still watched, and I still listened. Those buildings, that parking lot, and those people bustling around and living their lives held my sanity. Without them, I wouldn't exist; I wouldn't be able to sustain my mind. That, in itself, might sound insane to most, but I had no other words to describe it. I needed them, and I held on to them for as long as I could, until I heard the downstairs door open. There was another soft thud and then a crack, and I knew it to be the first step leading up the stairs. The old wooden staircase had seventeen steps, and I knew the sound made by each and every one of them.

There was another crack—three, four. I had to leave the outside behind, but every time it became harder to break away.

Five, six, I recognized every step, the way it shifted and buckled beneath the weight, the way the eighth step had a double crack every time—nine, ten.

A large bird that had settled on the carbon roof caught my eye, and for a second, I thought it might be watching me, but in the back of my mind, I knew that couldn't be possible. Twelve, thirteen, time to say good-bye—fourteen, fifteen. I blinked, and my eyes stung as if I had never used them before, sixteen.

My hands shook as I replaced the black foil that covered the window, careful to cover all the cracks and fissures until it expelled every shred of light, which left me shrouded in darkness.

Silence followed the seventeenth step and then came the footsteps along the hall. The footsteps got louder, and my breathing fell into the same rhythm. By touch, I crawled into the empty bathtub and crouched in a ball in the furthest corner. My body trembled, feeling the cold metal seep through my clothes as the footsteps came to a halt, and I closed my eyes.

Trying to focus on my breathing, I heard the click of the lamp outside the room. The light from the lamp would flicker and filter inside underneath the crack of the door, but I didn't dare to look.

Several locks clicked, and a latch scraped before I heard the door open. I didn't look —I didn't want to. I already knew the light behind him would shroud his figure in darkness, allowing me only to see the broad-shouldered frame, and he would always wear a hood. I knew the sight of the tall, dark figure far too well, and imagining it was enough. So I kept my eyes closed while heavy breathing filled the room.

I twitched at the loud clank of the metal plate landing on the floor. There was a scraping sound as the metal scratched along the stone tiles. It lifted a fraction of the uneasiness within my body, because it told me there wouldn't be any deviation from the routine, at least not that night.

If there were, he wouldn't have placed anything on the floor and would have just dragged me from my tub to the room with that dreaded chair. Although it didn't raise my confidence enough to release the tight grip on my legs—not until the door would shut. Breathing lingered in the room and made me hold my own breath, afraid to exhale, and I felt my lungs starting to burn.

"So sad," an almost kind voice said, but I knew this was how it started. First, his words would be soft-spoken—he had done it before on the few occasions he decided to speak.

"You're not even going to say hello," he said. "I thought you were better than this."

I wouldn't have thought it possible, but my muscles strained even further as if they were trying to protect themselves from the eventual blows, although with these blows he didn't mean to hurt my body—unlike other times, these blows he targeted at my mind. I didn't understand why he needed to torment me like this. He had me locked up inside this bathroom. *Wasn't that enough?* Besides, I had enough mental demons to deal with, without *his* added to the pile.

"Didn't your daddy teach you any

manners?" he spoke. "Maybe tonight we'll pay another visit to the chair and revisit some of those memories."

I wanted to scream to drown out his words. Covering my ears had never worked to keep his words from striking where they hurt. I forced myself to think. *This is impossible. He can't know about my father.* No one knew except for my mom. I had even kept it from you, my love. I had been so careful to keep that part of my life hidden. This had to be a coincidence—*he couldn't have known.* I repeated the word inside my mind until it turned into a slow rhythmic chant. "Coincidence… coincidence."

His voice lowered, but he spoke meticulously as he said, "Or didn't your daddy love you?"

I refused to listen. I had fought so hard to forget what had happened and even sacrificed a loving relationship with my mom, only so I could forget. Perhaps this did serve as punishment, as he wanted me to believe. Maybe I did deserve to be here, and this man acted as my jury, judge, and executioner.

"I know you can hear me, Julie, even if you pretend you don't, but I need you to cooperate, or else the story will never jump off the page," he said. "But don't worry. Soon I'll be able to give you some new incentive."

Only as I heard the footsteps leaving the room, the door closing, locks clicking and the latch sliding back into place, did I dare to breathe. At the time, I didn't know what he meant by incentive, and I wished I had never found out. After he had left, it took me several minutes to release my legs, and I remained still, lying alone in an empty tub, staring into darkness, trying to catch my breath.

Every day I said a prayer in the hope for a quiet night. I had never been a religious person, never went to church or lit a candle for someone in need, and I didn't think I had turned into one. Maybe I had become superstitious, or maybe I had been searching for something to comfort myself—anything to latch on to.

Mom had been the religious person in the family, and the few prayers I had known, I'd learn from her. I wondered, if she still said them, if I'd be in those prayers. I never wanted to be a person hypocritical enough to suddenly believe in a higher power by being in need. Still, in prayer it felt as if my mom was closer. I ached for my mom, yearning for her embrace, the touch of her arms folding around my shoulders, the slightest implication that I wasn't alone, and my mind wandered back to that dreadful day that had led me here.

Mom and I had had an argument that day. It seemed so stupid in hindsight, and I wished I could take it back. All she'd wanted was to come to my wedding, but I'd felt embarrassed, embarrassed by my mother living in a trailer park, embarrassed by the woman who raised me to be strong and who had taught me how to survive. She had denied herself anything just so she could give it to me, and I'd refused to let her come to my wedding. When the tears started to glisten in my mother's eyes, I'd felt the ache in my heart, but it hadn't stopped me from blaming my soon-to-be in-laws as the reason she couldn't come. That, of course, had been a lie. I'd hid my heritage from everyone I had met after leaving my home as I'd worked hard to provide for myself. I had barely scraped by, but that hadn't been something I could hide. My new family hadn't seemed to mind, even if they had made a fortune in real estate. I had rarely experienced the kindness that your parents bestowed upon me, and it was obvious they would never have held my heritage against me, if only my destitute past had been my true reason. I wanted to separate this new life from my old and didn't want you or your parents to find out about my secrets. My mother held those secrets and because of them had become too much of a reminder of what I had done.

That day, I'd dismissed my mother's tears, too occupied by the thoughts of posing for pictures in the beautiful wedding gown she would never see me wear. I had left my mom in tears, but I had forced the thought from my mind as I'd made my way home.

Somehow, it had felt as if I'd brought this upon myself. If I had only been able to ward off the ego fighting for my desire to fit in and had stayed with my mom that day as she had asked.

My mind started to tread into territories that I didn't want it to venture into. In those moments lying inside that darkness, I didn't want to be taken back, didn't want to be reminded of my old life, my friends, my stuff, and my love, and I forced myself to forget. That was how I had always done it, and that was why it had been hard for me to face my mom inside that trailer. It had brought about too many painful memories that I'd wanted to erase from my life. That's why it had remained hard for me to put them on the page, because what if you found out? I couldn't bear the thought of you finding out what I had done all those years ago and me not being the one who told you in person. It would have hurt you too much, and that would have broken me.

Roaming through those memories led me to wonder about how long I had been here. I couldn't cope with these thoughts during those tedious nights, and my mind fought to block them out. That didn't stop my mind from already knowing that it had been too long, too long for anyone to have kept hope alive. And if they hadn't—*what would that mean for me?* So I did what I always did. I rolled to my side, pulled my legs against my chest, and wrapped my arms around my head.

If I could, I would have ripped the thoughts from my mind with pliers and thrown them in a corner where the surrounding darkness could swallow them up. As he forces me to put these words on the page, I still feel the despair encompassing that answer. It was too late, though. The answer sat plastered in that picture behind the glass. Even though I had seen the changes in the weather of what must have been months, I refused to acknowledge them, but that day I had seen it in the mixture of clothes strutting along the street, some warm, but also light and bare. Not unlike the trees, naked but riddled with the fresh buds ready to blossom.

I remembered the sense of triumph I'd felt the day that I'd managed to peel the foil from the window for the first time. It seemed that moisture had found a way between the glass and the foil, and I'd managed to peel it away until it couldn't go any further, as if it were glued on, but there was just enough to see outside.

Snow had still covered the ground back then. I'd thought of managing to remove the foil as my mental escape—this connection to the world that would help keep my sanity, but as that hint of summer hung in the breeze, I'd regretted my decision. I had turned that perfect blue sky without a hint of the vast dark open space behind it into my own personal torture device. Perhaps insanity would have been the better choice.

That beautiful spring day, which should have been remembered in many ways, but not by the trail of tears sliding down my cheeks before I'd even realized I had been crying.

I hadn't allowed myself to cry inside this room for a long time, afraid of what the tears would have done to me and afraid of what the added sounds would have cost me. It was too late now, and I couldn't stop it, not unlike the child I once was, watching a movie about an old man trying to kill himself because the dog he'd loved had been taken away. The movie had been my mom's favorite, but it always broke my heart. I couldn't stop myself from crying then, and I couldn't stop myself at that moment inside that bathtub. I buried my head, ignored the salt and sour smells that permeated from my body, and cried. I cried for the months I'd spent in this room, I cried for the life I'd once had and for the love I had lost.

Chapter Three

Julie

Every waking moment spent inside that room felt as if it could have been my last. The certainty of dying alone inside this room grew stronger with each day. Wondering about how and when it would happen crowded my mind. Sometimes I even invited it. I practiced saying good-bye, especially as it came to you, and I hoped you could hear me. *But how would you know I had said it? Would you find out by cause of some miraculous intervention? Would you just know?* Of course not. Things like that didn't happen except in the movies, but then meeting you could have been a scene from a movie. Maybe not to others, but it felt like it to me —the same as all those movies I'd watched throughout the years, yearning to find that perfect person to spend the rest of my life with, to shed my fears of ending up alone.

As time passed, I had almost given up, until that day I'd found you. Now I realized it might all have been a facade, a promise of a better life, to break from the loneliness and abuse only to be sucked back in.

Belonging to you had made me feel alive, and I couldn't have been happier after you'd walked into that bookstore, the way you hid behind the display case of some writer's debut novel that first time we'd met. I had caught those sideway glances and felt the giddiness wash over me.

I had even lingered by the door after paying for my newest addition to the oversized bookcase, way too big for my tiny apartment. Casually turning back to the display case, I'd noticed you were gone, and I had felt my heart sink. Then had come the movie part that supposedly never happened in real life. The exchanging of a few looks had turned me to mush, and my hands had trembled, trying to get the change into my purse.

I had felt so foolish, not unlike a young schoolgirl with a crush, and you hadn't even been standing there anymore when the bag containing my newest possession had fallen to the ground. I had to bend over to pick it up, but you had already been there, smiling up at me.

Your dark hair had been styled in a deliberate shaggy manner as if you were some movie star pretending to convey that you just didn't care. Your face might have been plucked right from one of those billboards trying to sell you their overpriced wardrobe or fancy perfume, or maybe you just looked that way to me.

You had risen without taking your eyes off me, and I'd noticed your shaggy hair really was on purpose, carefully combed to hide ears that were a little too big and a touch too far from your head. I had not been able to help the smile from forming on my lips.

It had taken us from there, our roller-coaster ride of a lifetime, with dinners, picnics, meeting your family, and our monthly visit to that one particular bookstore. With a wedding on the horizon, it just couldn't get any better, and I hadn't conceived anything less, until I found myself sitting behind that glass, wondering if you had moved on.

Chapter Four

Julie

That next day, I jolted awake, my arms thrashing against the cold, hard surface of the bathtub before I remembered where I was. The stale, unfiltered air inside the bathroom invaded my lungs as I gulped deep breaths and forced myself to calm down. It seemed to take longer than usual to find my composure, to return to that person who tried to separate her mind from the harsh reality it lived in. Disentangling myself from my former life and the living seemed the only way to keep soundness of mind—to observe instead of participating.

I knew I hovered on the brink of insanity, and the one thing that kept me from screaming like a raving lunatic every morning were the repercussions. I had learned of them soon after I had arrived. Those first nights I had screamed and begged for someone to help me. Fighting my fears, I had tried to escape, but how does one pick a lock when there wasn't one to pick? The locks on the inside of the door had been removed. The person who had taken me, although he never showed his face, came to check on me usually twice a day— to bring the tray and to pick it up. One time, I had gone at him with that tray. Besides the fact that the act had taught me the room in which I was held captive must have been soundproofed to the outside world, I had also learned my limits. That night with the tray had left my right hand with two fingers that wouldn't properly bend anymore. He had broken them just to punish me.

An attempt to starve myself, for reasons I couldn't even fathom anymore, had robbed me of any courage or hope that I would be able to rescue myself. I hadn't known what was worse, the food forced down my throat as he had me sitting in that chair or the hammer he'd used on my knee to force my mouth to open.

The unwelcome memory sent a shiver down my spine, and then I remembered the tray. *Had I fallen asleep? How long have I been lying here?* My heart pounded in my throat, making it harder to register the sounds around me. If he came back before I finished the plate, he might think I had gone on a hunger strike again. The thought turned my body into a trembling mess. Forcing myself to listen, I heard nothing stir inside the house.

Slowly I crawled out of the bathtub, determined not to make a sound. The rough-tiled floor felt cold underneath my bare feet as I cowered at the side of the bathtub. I eased my hand out into the black void, careful not to bump into anything too hard. I didn't want to spill any of the food he had brought. On hands and knees, I shifted through the dark, feeling my way to the tray he had left on the floor.

Relief washed over me as I found the tray without tipping anything on it over. My fingers clamped around the glass, and my other hand sought out the stale bread. For the duration of my stay here, there had never been much variation in my diet, and I didn't expect any then. My nose had already caught a sour waft of odor coming from the milk gone bad. With no way of disposing of it, all the drains had been plugged, and I was allowed to flush the toilet once every so often after he'd removed the lock and examined its content—he would know if I were to throw it out. I knew I had to drink it one way or the other and force myself to keep it inside. Holding my breath, I set the glass to my mouth and started to gulp it down. My stomach heaved after the first swallow, but I forced it down. Swallow after swallow, the thick lumpy substance forced its way down my throat. Clamping my lips shut, I set the glass down and then slapped my hand over my mouth. As the initial reactions of my body refusing the vile content of the glass subsided, I thrust the stale bread into my mouth and chewed. As I chewed, I used my hand as a solid seal, refusing to throw up the sour milk that started to climb my throat. Back then, I couldn't fathom his reasons for slowly starving me this way, but the pictures staring back at me from the walls as I write these words inside this room seemed to hold the answer.

I was still chewing when my head shot up at a sound somewhere inside the house. I peered at the door I couldn't see in the darkness and held my breath. As if my body recognized the threat, my stomach stopped fighting the foul content it had to digest. My mind whirled. *Can it be morning already? Have I actually slept through the night?* I should cry more often if that made the terrifying sounds within the house fade into nothingness. The sounds of a door opening and closing made my blood run cold. Wood cracked as footsteps rose up the stairs. Still sitting on the floor, I scurried backward, scraping the fabric of my once-white cotton pants along the tiled floor until my back hit the bathtub.

As the light outside the bathroom clicked on and invaded the darkness inside, I settled back into the tub. My legs tugged against my chest, and my body started to quiver. I couldn't tell whether my stomach revolted or whether fear had grabbed hold of me, dreading a deviation in the routine. At the click of the door, I closed my eyes.

Heavy breathing filled the room,

footsteps, accompanied by the scrap of the tray on the tiles, a throat noise, and then the click of the door. I eased my eyes open and saw the light disappear from underneath the door. A sliver of relief ran along my body as a breath escaped passed my lips. The realization that there wouldn't be a deviation from the routine made me breathe a little easier. He hadn't even taken the time to hurt me with his words. This would mean I'd have the rest of the day to myself and be able to connect with the outside from behind the glass.

Chapter Five

Julie

As I sat in my usual spot on the toilet, peering out through the hole where I had removed the layer of foil from the glass, I managed to calm my nerves. It had taken a while after the last click of the door and the rattling of the keys for me to drag myself from the bathtub. I'd wanted to be sure that I was alone.

I had managed to peel the foil from the glass enough that I could see through without tearing it too much. I had perfected the task of removing the foil and replacing it exactly as it had been before; it had become an obsession to me. The thought of him finding out what I did after he left would turn my stomach, but the thought of spending my days in the dark scared me

more. The sun sat at an angle, stretching its rays to reach the Victorian buildings beyond the parking lot. A sobering gray haze loomed over the structures but accompanied by an anticipation of a spring day.

The parking lot had gained some vehicles since the last time I'd looked. The environmentally friendly car had remained in its spot. The world before me seemed quiet for the longest time, and I wondered if it might be Sunday, until a gate across the street opened. An elderly gentleman stepped through. The word *gentleman* only loosely fitted the man's description, because in his sandals, gracefully filled with knitted socks and with his shorts underneath a blue overcoat, it looked as if he wore a skirt.

I couldn't help a smirk as the man pushed a moped past the gate and set it on its stand. He put on a helmet that squashed his face into a wrinkled mush of lines and creases. He topped off his creation with a pair of solid black shades that you would expect on a rough biker. The man kick-started the moped, almost plunging over before he sat his butt on the seat. The little engine rattled to life as he started rolling down the street.

I leaned back, feeling the cold tiles through the fabric of my flimsy shirt and pulled my legs to my chest. As always, my bad knee throbbed, but I ignored it as I wrapped my arms around it. Sharp bony knees connected with the pointed elbows of my arms, skin over bone that was all that was left of me—courtesy of being on a diet of stale bread and sour milk for months'.

My eyes followed the scarce light filtering through my only connection to the world outside and peered into the lifting darkness of the bathroom. The room stood in contrast to what it should have been or to what I wanted it to be. A room used for holding someone against her will, in my mind, should resemble a dungeon or any other dank place, but nothing similar to this.

Expensive-looking black and white tiles covered the floor. An antique bathtub hovered over those tiles and stood on shiny pedestals cornered against the wall. The room also contained a sink and a massive walk-in shower. Gold knobs would have provided the means to turn on the water if he hadn't disconnected them. Although the rest of the room had been stripped bare, it was the type of bathroom I might have been jealous of, flipping through the pages of some gossip or fashion magazine.

I hadn't seen much of the house except the bathroom, but what I had seen of the materials used for the interior reeked of wealth. The few times my captor had released me from my private residence, he had dragged me to a separate room on this same floor.

Fear still grabbed me as I remembered the first time he'd taken me there. I had never been that scared in my life. Well, maybe when hands had grabbed me and pulled me from my bike just before I'd felt the needle plunge into my neck, but that had been over quick. Since that first time inside that room on that chair, my fear seemed to multiply with every visit.

The first time that he'd changed his routine, the door to the bathroom had opened, and there hadn't been a plate of food shoved inside. My body had trembled, and tears had run down my cheeks as he'd tied my hands behind my back. I'd screamed, but he had silenced me with a smack across my face. Sometimes I thought I could still feel the burning sensation on my cheek and his breath on my ear as he spoke in a businesslike tone.

He'd said, "No one can hear you scream but me, and you do not wish to anger me." His voice had been so deep and low, with a little rasp, which had made him sound even more menacing. I couldn't imagine a face with the voice, but the ease with which he'd pull me to my feet and dragged me down a darkened hallway convinced me he had to be young and in the prime of his life.

I'd wanted to focus, wanted to figure out where I was, familiarize myself with my surroundings as if I could somehow help myself. I had seen enough scary movies that I thought I knew what to look for. It had been one of my favorite pastimes. I had curled up into your strong arms and pretended to be scared. As it often did in these reminiscing moments, a tear had escaped from the corner of my eye, and I'd pushed the memory of you from my mind.

My pay-per-view subscription had been upgraded, and now I'd had to live inside my own scary movie, and there hadn't been any place in it for you.

My knees had scraped the floor as he dragged me across the solid wooden boards. I had passed several doors on my left, and the stairs had come up on my right. The hallway had seemed to continue forever, and the boards had creaked underneath my bare feet. He had held me by my neck, forcing my head down, and I hadn't been able to see much beyond the floor and cream-colored walls.

My heart had raced against my chest, and I hadn't been able to breathe. Possibilities had flashed through my mind, increasing my fear. The cream-colored walls had made room for decorative wood paneling in some places, but I hadn't detected any furniture, lamps, or trinkets. Similar to the bathroom, the place had felt like old money, as if I was staying at one of those Victorian buildings across the street.

At the end of the hall outside that final

door, I had lost it. I had thrashed against his grip, surprising him, because his hands had faltered for a second, and I'd pulled myself free, but we had stood at the end of the hallway with nowhere left to go, and my hands had been bound behind my back. I'd felt the jab of his fist in my stomach and had fallen to my knees, gasping for air. Spots had flashed across my eyes, but the pain had quickly subsided after I'd felt the familiar sting of a needle in the side of my neck.

I must have regained consciousness somewhere along the way, because I vaguely remembered sitting in an awkward position. The room around me had been dark, like the bathroom, and I'd felt cold—so cold.

Fabric had wrapped around my neck, draping down my back and naked body. One of my arms had been raised high over my head, pinned by chains or ropes, and my legs had sat folded underneath me. Bright flashes had filled the room. At first, I'd thought it to be a thunderstorm, but there had been no thunder, only the bright flashes. My hair hung loose, obscuring my vision, and something kept me from raising my head. I couldn't make sense of it. The light had hurt my eyes after having been in the dark for too long, and I'd closed them. I couldn't remember much after that, so I presumed that I must have passed out.

Afterward, it hadn't seemed as if anything else had happened, but I couldn't know for sure. Scribbling on this page, I fear the answer to what had happened to be obvious, but my fear stops me from confronting the framed faces hanging from the surrounding walls and keep my head down.

As I sat on that toilet that memory and the ones that followed made me tighten the grip around my legs.

Chapter Six

Matthew

Was it you? The black-and-white picture plastered on my computer screen showed the once perfectly toned body that belonged to an unrecognizable woman. In a million years, I wouldn't have connected this fragile fragment of a person with you—the woman I wanted to spend the rest of my life with. I couldn't imagine your athletically built body, the dark-brown, curly hair that would fight you in a heavy breeze, making you wish it were straight, reduced to a shadow on the wall.

He demanded that I conveyed these thoughts into the written word, but how could I ever translate how seeing your fragile form on the screen had made me feel. Those bright, golden-brown eyes that would light up my life every day and would never falter. Nothing could break your strength or waver your independence, even after all the shit life had offered to you. Landing at rock bottom, you would get up, brush yourself off, and stand taller. This is how I had come to know you, and with what your mother had told me, this was why I then refused to believe that this half-naked woman, skin over bones, with her legs awkwardly bent, one hand chained to the ceiling while the other sat strapped to her back, was you.

The black-and-white picture didn't match your beautiful, olive-colored skin. Hell, nothing in this picture resembled you in any way, but after two weeks of scrutinizing that dreadful image, to the point that it had become an obsession—or maybe it had been the moment that I first saw it and recognized those two tiny details—I couldn't get the thought out of my head that this had to be you.

I clearly remembered the first time I'd noticed the small, half-moon-shaped birthmark on your back. We'd been dating for a couple of weeks, and you had spent the night at my place. You'd lain stretched out on my bed, your face buried in my pillow, and I'd felt the urge to explore.

I'd gently pulled down the covers to

reveal your naked shoulders. You hadn't stirred, but I had been able to tell you were awake. I had always been able to tell by the rhythm of your breathing. At the time, I hadn't known whether you'd known, but I had. I'd known then that you were mine, and I would never let you go. As these words find their way onto this page, I can only pray for that reality.

The back of my hand had gently followed the length of your spine until it had derailed onto the curve of your hip. My lips had found the small of your back and slowly made their way down. That was when I'd found it. Just like the picture, the birthmark shaped as a half-moon had just peeked out from under your lacy, black underwear. Unable to resist temptation, I'd kissed it.

You had chuckled and turned to face me, looking through sleep-deprived eyes, but with a smile that had thrown me aback.

"What are you doing?" you'd said in that raspy voice you carried in the mornings.

"Marking my territory," I'd replied. "That...right here...is mine."

I had grinned at your mischievous smile and made my way up, kissing the curves of your body until I'd found your lips.

This tiny birthmark, along with a scar that poked out from behind your ear, had created the seed for my doubts. You had always gracefully diverted my questions about the scar, but after talking with your mother, I'd wished I had never brought it up. Two distinct features belonging to you reflected back at me from the screen, two features that didn't seem to belong on this broken body, and yet there they were.

I missed you, Julie. I missed you more with every second that passed on the clock. My friends had told me I'd lost my mind, aching for a sign that you were okay and that you would come back to me. They'd told me you'd left, that you had played me, but to what end? Except for some clothes, everything you owned still sat at our place. One of those friends had said you'd probably run away out of shame, because of what I had learned about your mother living in a trailer park, but you hadn't even known

I had found out yet. Neither had you known of the things your mother had told me, and I would never divulge those secrets to anyone.

Although I'd never bought my friend's explanations, they had toyed with my mind, but that picture had challenged those doubts on a grander scale. This was too much to bear, and I felt afraid to imagine what this would mean for you if it were true.

The subtitle underneath the picture read: *The pitiful-hearted and the dying.* According to the site where I'd found the picture, it belonged to a set of two, both of the same woman, but I hadn't built up the courage to scroll down to the second image, not even in the two weeks that had passed after finding the first one.

A friend of a friend had recommended the photographer, and in my line of work, I could always use a fresh new artist to fill the empty pages of the glossy magazine I worked for. Within the first clicks after arriving on the website, I'd known this man wasn't a fresh new artist.

A range of five series, containing pictures

that the so-called artist described as a peek into the lines between the living and the dead, had found a prominent spot on the man's page. All five series contained a set of photographs, and a different woman posed for a set of five pictures in each series. Back then it hadn't occurred to me that there had been only two pictures in your series, but I doubt it would have made a difference in finding you.

The pictures of the half-naked skin-over-bone women strapped into the most awful, torturous contraptions had caused much controversy in the art world. Some had raised questions about the state of the unrecognizable women in the pictures; others had complained about their violent nature. About the women's conditions, the photographer himself had explained it away with the fact that some of the women had been physically ill but had been happy to immortalize themselves in the name of art.

Others had raised issues about the picture of a woman with her arm stretched so far back that it had looked as if her shoulder had dislocated. The photographer had written it off as a visual effect. This, of course, was a viable explanation with the software available these days. The names of the models had remained undisclosed because of the nature of their illnesses or out of respect for their families and, of course, the contract they had signed.

"Fucking pervert" were the first words that had crossed my mind, clicking through the pictures on the man's site. I had no idea what that friend of a friend had been thinking when he'd recommended the site to me, and I would have told him he had a sick mind, but then I'd found that particular picture.

I had confronted my friend Dennis and had demanded he tell me who had recommended this so-called photographer, but he'd refused my request. After I had practically begged him to reveal this person's identity so I could talk to him, our confrontation had quickly escalated. Dennis had refused to tell me. He'd kept arguing that it wouldn't be ethical to reveal his source, as if he had been protecting a client. In retrospect, my state of mind might have had something to do with it. My intentions might have been to beg for information, but from Dennis's statement to the police, it seemed I had come on too strong, and it had taken him aback. Your disappearance and the discovery of that picture had broken something inside me, and it had become impossible to keep my emotions in check.

After I punched him in the nose, he'd called the cops on me. Apparently, Dennis hadn't been the friend I'd thought he was, or perhaps he feared what I would do to that certain someone after I'd gotten my hands on him. I had gotten him to spill that it might have been someone I also had known. After that, a restraining order had kept me from going near him again.

I might not have known where the recommendation originated or whom it had come from, but it had set me on a course to find that photographer.

It all had gone so fast after that, the changes in my life, moving across the country to hunt a man who might or might not have abducted you. It had sped up like a roller coaster that had brought me to my new apartment in a different state in search of a sign that you were okay.

Chapter Seven

Matthew

For the briefest moment after you disappeared, I had felt so angry with you, but how could I have known? For weeks, I had wandered around the office like a zombie, performing my tasks on autopilot. Of course, working on automatic pilot in a job that demanded the right amount of creativity hadn't been enough. Six weeks into your disappearance, my boss, Hank, had called me into his office. I couldn't blame him for not being satisfied with my work. Hell, I hadn't been satisfied. I hadn't been able to concentrate; you had been all I could think off. For someone who thought that my fiancé had recently left me, Hank had been amiable enough. He'd sent me home for the rest of the week, and I had rewarded him by not returning the next Monday. All I had known was that you were gone. You hadn't come home, and all this on the day that I'd found out you had lied to me.

You had lied to me about everything. Well, maybe not lied, but you had left things out. We had been supposed to get married, and you had never even told me that your mother had been still alive.

Shame still grabbed me as I thought of that day I'd followed you. Trust had come easily to me, especially concerning you, but you'd had this ritual once a month that you had never wanted to explain. You would take the afternoon off and then go... somewhere. Although it had never made me doubt your love, it had bothered me. It had bothered me because we were supposed to get married, and to me, that meant not keeping any secrets. I had known that trust hadn't come easily to you, but you could have told me about your mother, and I wished you had told me about your demons. You hadn't needed to battle them alone, not anymore. The fights your mother had fought for you and you for her made me love you even more. But you hadn't trusted me enough to tell me.

Chapter Eight

Matthew

I never intended to put these words to the page. My conversation with your mother should never see the light of day, and I feel ashamed to be the one to out you like this, but what am I supposed to do? The choice has been taken away from me. Perhaps you would someday forgive me for not being strong enough to keep your secret.

On the inside, the trailer looked more spacious than I would have thought. Your mother had crafted a cozy little nest, and although the smell of burned-out cigarettes lingered in the rectangular space, I could tell she kept it tidy with pride. As she guided me inside, the way you resembled each other became evident, but the sorrow that lingered on her face had added years to her appearance.

I noticed your visit had left your mother with puffy cheeks and red-glazed eyes. She watched me in awe as I explained my visit, and once she figured out who I was to you, she burst into tears. I wanted to console her but didn't know how—didn't even think she wanted me to. Words spilled from her mouth, starting with the reason that had left her in tears in the first place. She wanted me to apologize to my parents for not meeting their expectations, and she didn't blame them for not wanting her to attend her daughter's wedding. It took some discipline on my part to keep from defending my family and tell her that they didn't even know she existed. I feared it might be too painful to find out her daughter had feigned her dead.

Your mother just wanted someone to hear her side of the story, and as she revealed it, I could understand your reluctance to revisit the memories of that life.

She said, "I never thought she had it in her...you know?" I sensed the quiver in your mother's voice and understood her story could not be rushed. I let her take her time. "Because I never could have done it."

I could sense her reluctance, as if she

weren't sure whether she could trust me. Her eyes roamed over me like a hawk, but for some reason, she must have thought me trustworthy and continued.

She said, "The police had released Jim, my ex and Julie's father, only an hour before he appeared on our doorstep." She shook her head in disgust. "The bastard had cracked the back of Julie's head, and those cops just let him go on account of some dumb technicality after only a couple of weeks in the slammer."

She must have read the shock on my face, and before she continued her story, she grabbed a bottle of cheap vodka, which it turned out I needed.

She refilled the glass I had just thrown back while she continued her tale. She explained how the loss of his job and too much alcohol had turned her husband into the abusive man he had become. It would usually be her who caught the brunt of his rage, but as you entered her teens and flourished into a beautiful young woman, you had captured his attention—especially when she stepped up to protect her mom.

"I didn't know where the gun had come from, but I knew Jim would have killed us both if she hadn't done what she did."

She said it so matter-of-factly that it seemed as if she reported a news fact. I, however, nearly choked on the vodka. After a coughing fit, I said, "Julie shot him."

I stared at her in disbelief. This couldn't be true. I knew you, and the Julie I knew wouldn't be capable of such an act. The incredulity and doubt must have been evident on my face, because tears started to flood her eyes as she said, "You don't understand. The man went crazy the moment he arrived, accusing us of betrayal and screaming like a lunatic. Not a single piece of furniture was left unturned, most of the dishes had to be replaced, and several windows were broken..." She took a deep breath as she paused. "She shot him three times, but—"

Your mother broke herself off as if the memories of it all were too much. Shaking fingers reached for the pack of cigarettes on the table, and as she lit one, our eyes reconnected, but she didn't seem to look at me, as if her gaze went straight through me.

She said, "Even with two bullets in his torso, he kept shouting that he was going to fucking kill us. He shouted it over and over again until that third shot."

Overcome with guilt, she started to rant. "I should have done it, I should have been the one, but I couldn't get off the floor. My baby was sixteen years old and had to shoot her daddy in the head to keep us safe."

Silence filled the trailer as your mother stared off into a corner of the room, with a smoldering cigarette in her hand. As the facts of your horrific childhood filtered in, I wondered if your mother's eyes lingered on the spot where your dad had died or if you had been standing there. I pictured you ten years younger, standing over the body of your dead father, holding a gun in your hand. The image sent a chill down my spine, and I shivered.

With a refilled glass of vodka in my hand, your mother explained how that last shot had nearly killed your future as well. How the police hadn't bought their story and had arrested you, that there weren't any technicalities that time, and that it had ended with them shipping you to a mental facility.

It had taken some time, but eventually the courts had acquitted you, and you'd managed to pick up your life. I couldn't imagine how hard it must have been for you, and I felt so proud of the woman you had become. I even understood the reasons for you hiding your mother's existence, although I doubted it had anything to do with her.

We sat and spoke for a long time after that—your mother and me. It took everything I had to keep me from scrambling home so I could throw my arms around you, but your mom convinced me I shouldn't rush into divulging to you everything I had learned. She was right, though. There had been a reason you had tried to scrub it all clear from your ledger, but I still wished I had gone to find you when I still had the chance.

Chapter Nine

Julie

Those times as the house sat empty, it somehow seemed to move quietly in its places. It was as if the house was alive and talked to me, but I refused to understand. I knew all the cracks and ticks of the of the old wood responding to moist, heat, and wind, so why did I jump every time the house spoke? Especially trapped in darkness, I could sense the noises conjured inside my head chip away at my sanity and I felt my mind slip. Only that feeble connection to the world outside would help me from going insane, and imagining that the house might eat me alive.

The early sunlight peeked through the hole I had made by peeling the foil from the window. The world outside was still fast asleep, and I didn't want to think about this house. I needed a distraction, something to take my mind off the creaking noises made by a house, unable to deal with its emptiness, something that would keep my mind from wandering in a direction where it turned the sounds into ghosts, and I lost my mind completely. *Why couldn't a neighbor be out yet so I could observe him or her?* Just as I had observed you as you sat behind your computer.

I used to love to watch you work. The way your fingers clacked the keyboard and the focus you held as your eyes roamed the screen. You had found the job you had always dreamed of, and although I felt a pang of jealousy at the stacks of papers claiming your attention, I never dared to intervene. Browsing through pictures of the most beautiful women in the world, finding them a spot on the page, came with your job, and I didn't have to like it, but I forced myself to keep it separated from the life we shared. Maybe it came out of fear that you would leave me if I claimed more of your time, so I just sat there and watched until you finished—hoping your focus would soon fall on me. *Had you lost your focus on me since the last time you had seen me?*

The thought filled my chest with pain,

and I soon searched for something else to occupy my mind beyond the glass.

Rays of sun bounced off a window across the street and sent a beam of focused light inside my bathroom. Either *he* had left earlier than usual, or the earlier sunrise caused the reflecting light to penetrate my prison more brightly than it had in the days before. The focused stream of sunlight didn't add much light to my darkened surroundings, but it gave my eyes the relief of seeing some additional features of the room. Fear that I had gone blind shocked me awake regularly, especially in the early days spent inside that room.

My eyes followed the beam of sunlight to where it stopped on the frame of the door. I squinted as my eyes adjusted and I gasped at something I hadn't noticed before. My heart pounded, and I felt a tremor return to my hands. Shaking like a leaf, I slid off the toilet and crawled along the cold floor to the door. My knee ached, but I refused to take my eyes of the little patch of light.

I stretched out a shaky finger to touch

the wooden frame as if feeling it would confirm the truth of what I saw—letters carved into the wood. Feeling the indents underneath the tips of my finger sent a shiver down my spine. I found a letter H and slightly below that an A and an N. I cringed and nearly gagged at the sight of a fingernail wedged into the letter N. I tried to breathe, but it was as if my lungs refused the air I wanted to give them.

"Oh God, oh God," I said in a soft chant as if they were the only words I knew. My eyes fell on a few darkened specks against the white paint. It could have been anything, but I knew. I knew it had to be blood. I wanted to scream but managed to place a hand over my lips. Although he wasn't even in the house, he had trained me well to keep my mouth shut. In my mind, I couldn't allow myself to scream—the fear of repercussions was too overwhelming. I scrambled backward fast and sudden, until my head connected with the wall underneath the window. As I made myself as small as I could, sitting under the fading beam of sunlight, I could only repeat those two same words from before. "Oh God, oh God." I couldn't stop shaking as the reality of it sank in.

There had been others.

Chapter Ten

Matthew

You had left me—that was the consensus among our friends. This could have something to do with the fact that most of them were my friends from before we'd met. You had always been a hard person to reach, even for me, but once you'd let me in, I'd never doubted the tenderness inside your soul, although others had found it hard to connect with you. It hadn't been hard for me to accept this side of you as long as you hadn't shut me out. That is why I'd felt so angry with you when I'd first learned your mother still lived.

I had never believed, unlike many others, that you would pack up and leave without saying good-bye. I grew frustrated with the police when they dropped your case after only two months and had almost gotten myself arrested by shoving a detective in the shoulders. Nothing indicated foul play, and it seemed as if you had left on your own accord. There had been no evidence of any kind except that some of your clothes were missing from our apartment and at that point, I hadn't found those pictures yet. This all led the police to the conclusion that you had left me.

I tried to convince my family, and I think my mother supported my beliefs, for the most part, those first months, especially after I told her your story and what happened with your mother, although I didn't delve into details about your father, but in the end, she just seemed to humor me. She recognized the pain I felt and wanted to comfort me. Eventually, your mother became my rock. Your mother was convinced something had happened to you, as was I; you wouldn't just leave without a word. You might have left me, but you would never have left your mother, not after what the two of you had lived through.

Through her convictions, I felt certain that I would see you again, and those pictures posted on the net confirmed it, although they added despair to my fears and desires to find you.

Had it been this despair that had driven me to the acts of stupidity that have led me here? Had my desire to find you left me without the ability to think? But I guess everything seems obvious in hindsight.

The wooden floorboards cracking behind me and his footsteps closing in drew my attention to my friend Scott.

He said, "I must say, Matt, quite the place you got here." As his deep voice opened up, I turned my chair so I could face him, and he handed me a beer. "Still not sure about the reasoning"—he crossed the room and eased himself onto the couch —"but I wish you had called me and not your mom."

I hadn't called anyone. Why would I? Hell, most of my friends had thought me insane, and I couldn't stand the pity-filled eyes of my family members any longer. Besides, I had found a lead—a clue that might bring you back to me. It hadn't taken me long to find the photographer, and two weeks after I had first laid eyes upon that picture, with almost six months into your disappearance, I had found an apartment in an old Victorian building across from his home.

I said, "Why, so you could have talked me out of it?"

Scott leaned back, balancing the beer on his knee. "Probably," he replied, "but after realizing I wouldn't be able to, I could have been here sooner."

I smiled at my friend who, ever since elementary school, had always had my back, although it seemed odd that my mother had contacted Scott. She had never particularly liked him and had continually tried to convince me that something had changed him ever since he had gotten back from his two tours in Afghanistan especially after the fight I had with her about what she'd called "following your ghost across the country." She'd thought my decision rash, and I hadn't thought she'd nourish my beliefs by asking Scott to help me. Maybe she just wanted someone to keep an eye on me. Knowing my mom, besides my wellbeing, she had probably feared I was wasting my money. My parents had worked hard to reach a level where they didn't have to worry about money anymore, and they wouldn't tolerate me squandering it. Fortunately, they had raised me well, and although I had quit my job without finding another one after my move, along with the added rent of this new place, I had a considerable amount of savings. As much as I liked a certain level of comfort, I wasn't in the habit of wasting money.

Especially after I had met you, who jokingly called me a "spoiled little rich kid" as I'd complained about having to do some chore instead of hiring a cleaning lady. You had made me aware of how lucky I had been. You'd taught me to be more grateful for the little things in life. Although my parents had their doubts that something other than you leaving had happened to you, they continued to support me, if only because they knew, how important you were to me. Whatever my mother's reason for calling Scott might have been, I appreciated his presence.

"How long have you been stateside?" I

asked.

"A while," he replied. Scott's eyes never left the bottle of beer as he spun it around its axis.

"So what have you been up to?" I asked reluctantly. After his second tour, Scott had spent a significant time in the hospital, recovering from an injury. During that time, he had refused visitors, and after they'd released him, he had told me he wanted to see the better things this world had to offer.

He said, "Oh...this and that, traveled a bit, worked a couple of jobs—you know, scraping by." Scott hadn't been that fun-loving kid he had been while growing up for a long time, but he was my friend, and I didn't want to push him for answers he didn't want to give.

Scott's gaze redirected to the computer screen behind me where the picture still stood on display. His face appeared impassive, as if he couldn't see beyond the black and white and didn't recognize the horror before his eyes.

He said, "What are you hoping for

here?" He took a swig from his beer and then shook his head as he rose from the couch. He walked across the room to where I sat behind the desk. "I know you think that's her and all," he said as he stopped next to me, "but it seems to me this could be anyone."

Annoyed at his implication that I wouldn't be able to recognize the woman I was supposed to marry, I shot him an angry look and said in a defensive tone, "It's her. I know it is."

Scott lifted his bottle in defeat before he took another swig and then said, "But the police never denied or confirmed it."

"They said that the photographer's background papers checked out, but because of the confidentiality contracts signed by the models, they wouldn't be able to divulge any identities," I replied, trying to retain some calm in my voice. "They said Julie wasn't among them, and they had no indication that it was actually her in the pictures, but if I wanted to know more, then I should take it up with the photographer."

"So none of this has raised any suspicion?" Scott added, along with a throat noise that might have sounded a little stunned. I couldn't tell him about your own encounter with the law and how it had hurt your creditability within the system, so I gave Scott the version I had given everyone.

"Everything points to Julie leaving on her own account," I said, "and I don't think my harassing the police helped matters." Guilt washed over me as I remembered how I barked at that detective. Overcome by anger, I had grabbed his jacket and shoved him against the wall. The callousness in his attitude had just gotten to me, and I'd lost it. Fortunately, he hadn't pressed any charges, but the detective also hadn't helped me plead your case when I came to the photographer's hometown after I asked the local chief of police to contact him. Tracking the photographer to a different state hadn't made things easier.

My gaze returned to the picture while Scott remained by my side. I took a calming breath and was ready to reach for the mouse to close the site when Scott spoke. "You should scroll down. There's another picture."

I said, "No." The word came out louder than I'd meant to.

He pointed his bottle at the screen and said, "Dude, I know it's not pretty, and her face is still obscured, but it's at a different angle, and it might give us—or should I say you—some new clues."

That was it. Maybe my mom had been right, and something was wrong with Scott.

I said, "Are you kidding me? Clues?" As I looked up to face him, Scott seemed taken aback by my reaction, but it didn't stop him from adding something else.

"We need all the information we can get, and it would be nice to have our facts straight before we decide to commit a felony." His words rushed out in a defensive tone. "Besides, you have an eye for pictures —you might see things I'd miss."

"Those are all the clues I need," I said in too loud a voice. With a finger, I pointed at the picture and specifically at the scar that poked out from behind your ear.

Before he could reply, I clicked the cross on the browser to close the screen. To a rational, thinking person, his words might have made sense, but I had left thinking rationally behind about six months ago. Quenching the anger that stirred in my gut, I pushed my chair from the desk. The plastic wheels scrapped the hard wooden floor until I forced them to stop.

I said, "Why don't you tell me what you have in mind?" Although I felt frustrated by my friend's reaction, I figured he might not know how I felt about you. For all I knew then, you two had only met once and that at a crowded party at my parents' place before Scott had left for his second tour. It reminded me of how you had told me about feeling intimidated by the broad-shouldered soldier and how you couldn't picture us being friends except for the interest he conveyed in my parents' art collection. You mentioned he had an eye for it, but I couldn't imagine him having any appreciation for disturbing pictures like these, even though someone had labeled them art.

Scott said, "Right, sorry, I didn't mean to upset you."

I said, "Forget about it." All I wanted was to get you back into my life, and if Scott's help meant I had to deal with his dense remarks, I could live with that.

"Let's get started," I said as I pushed my chair back to the desk.

Scott absently nodded, but he had this determined look on his face that I interpreted as him wanting to do anything in his power to help me. But I could have been wrong about that.

"Exactly. Let's find our girl," he said a moment later as he placed his hand on my shoulder. I glanced up at him wondering if he truly believed it to be you in those pictures, but I couldn't read his expression. "Let me get my stuff. I'll be back in a sec." Scott turned on his heels and headed to the kitchen. "It's a good thing that this building has easy access from the back of the house— keeps us from getting noticed."

As he walked, I noticed Scott still had that soldier's strut—straight as a pole, with a firm step that must have sounded like cannonballs to the downstairs neighbors every time his boots hit the floor. I could still hear him in the hall outside the apartment as he made his way down the old staircase.

I felt stupid for not telling Scott sooner—I should've known he would help. I didn't want him to think I was going insane. Of course, I still had my doubts about it being you in that picture, although I knew it came out of fear of it being you. It wasn't easy to decide what felt worse, knowing it was you in those dreadful pictures or remaining in the dark to what had happened to you.

Despite my doubts and Scott's misgivings, I had felt grateful for his help and military mind. If it turned out to be you in that picture, there wouldn't be anyone better to help me get you out. If you were still alive.

Chapter Eleven

Matthew

Scott had set up a stakeout worthy of a CIA sting operation. High-definition recording devices, laptops, night vision goggles, and other sophisticated-looking long-range observation equipment sat centered on my desk. He told me he had rented most of the stuff, and I should be expecting a significant bill. I didn't care as long as I got you back.

Using the equipment, Scott kept a constant eye on the place across the street, only diverting from the scope to make some notes or to download pictures onto the computer to get a better look. I pretty much felt useless, bringing in the occasional plate of food and refreshments.

Along with the floor plans he had managed to dig up and his observations, Scott had drawn up a detailed scheme of the massive brownstone across the street.

He focused on what he described as the hotspots, which included the front and back door, a blacked-out window at the front that, according to our floorplan, was supposed to be a bathroom, and a blacked-out window at the back that could be a bedroom, but Scott believed it to be a study or a workplace.

In any other case, someone might have perceived it strange for a house to have windows darkened by some type of material, but the fact a fairly well-known photographer owned the place made it acceptable. Even in this digital age, it was probable that a photographer might need a darkroom.

On the man taking the pictures, we couldn't find much information except for what he wanted us to know according to his website profile and the tales spun by his publicist. Supposedly, he worked from his home where he developed his pictures, but he usually did his photo shoots in a warehouse near the docks.

In the first week after I had moved into my new place, I had followed him to that warehouse several times. The place had buzzed with people on a few occasions.

Some type of catering company had attended to a group of people carrying around equipment and other stuff. Others had sat around as they'd waited to be catered to. From my own experience on photo shoots, it hadn't been hard to figure out those were the models. On other times I had followed him, the building had sat abandoned except for his car standing in front of the entrance. I had debated entering the building, but considering the trouble I'd already had concerning the police in the previous months, I had abandoned the idea.

That morning our photographer had left his house early, earlier than he usually did. As we had observed for the past two days and the time since I had moved in, we knew him to leave at around nine o'clock and to return at dusk. This aberration in his routine had my mind whirling, and I wanted to follow him to see what he was up to, but Scott advised against it. He argued that I had been lucky not to have been spotted the first few times I had followed the photographer. Now that I had been living here for a while, Scott thought the man might recognize my car or even me if I followed him too often. I doubted it, but reluctantly I agreed.

Scott wanted to focus on observing the house and its surroundings so we could enter it without running into too much trouble. He also wanted to act soon, and I had to agree with that. *Who knew how long ago that picture had been taken and how much your body might have suffered since then?*

As time ticked by and Scott did his thing, I couldn't draw my eyes from the brownstone across the street. By now, I knew every detail of the house—the cracks in the stone steps that led up to the massive wooden door and the high-framed windows that appeared uninviting because the curtains were always drawn. Ivy crawled up on the right side of the door all the way up to the blacked-out window where it suddenly seemed to stop. Except for the ivy, the place seemed well managed. There wasn't a crack in the paint in sight.

Although we couldn't see the rear of the house directly, Scott had managed to place cameras in the backyard, and they gave us a good view. The photographer had left the apartment at the crack of dawn and Scott had taken his time setting things up. Tonight, he'd go back to check them and see whether anyone might have spotted or tinkered with them.

Observing the backyard didn't show us anything out of the ordinary. Just as any fine place owned by rich people, the backyard appeared well manicured, with a beautiful grass lawn and trimmed bushes. The only thing that seemed strange, but similar to the front, was that the curtains were always drawn. No one in the neighborhood seemed to question the fact.

When I asked around, my neighbors had told me the man living in the house was a little eccentric and liked his privacy. None of them acted suspicious of the photographer, but his pictures—these abominations he had created—told me better.

As I watched the house, uneasiness

started to build inside me. *How were we to learn anything if we couldn't see what was going on inside the house? How could we find out if you were in there?* I felt useless waiting around for Scott to do his thing.

Unnerved, I turned with the aim to find something to drink in the kitchen, but I stopped as I caught a glance over Scott's shoulder. He sat at my desk, scrutinizing the computer screen, and the image it displayed sent a shock through my body.

I said, "What the hell are you doing?" Scott barely moved his head at the sound of my voice, and without taking his eyes from the screen, he asked, "What?"

I stomped across the room, the sound of my boots loud on the wooden floor. My heart hammered painfully in my chest, and tears filled my eyes as the image on the screen came into focus. The overexposed shape in the middle of the picture seemed to levitate in the surrounding darkness. Arms and legs pointed up as if hanging by an invisible rope with uneven length. A puppet on strings was what it reminded me of for the briefest of seconds, but then I saw eyes covered by black cloth and a mouth contorted into a scream. Your face was still obscured, but it was you.

Anger surged through my veins as I reached the desk and shouldered Scott out of my way. He grunted as his chair rolled to a side.

He said, "What is wrong with you?"

Unable to listen, I fumbled for the mouse, but my adrenaline-spiked brain wouldn't allow me to think, and I couldn't get the screen to close. This image could not be the last thing of you in my memory. In a last desperate effort to stop this picture taking up permanent residence inside my mind, I grabbed the flat screen and slammed it on the desk.

Behind me, I heard Scott sigh. I drew in a breath of my own to calm my nerves. *For how long has he been staring at that picture?* He hadn't even flinched as I'd called out to him, engrossed by the displayed terror. Anger reigned over my body as I turned to look at him and spoke. "Why would you do that? I told you I wasn't ready to see that."

Scott said, "You'd never be ready to see that, but I need to be sure that this isn't some artistic expression."

"Did that look like an artistic expression?" I replied, raising my voice. "That is an abomination and has no artistic value whatsoever."

Scott winced and then frowned as he said, "Chill out Matt, many others seem to think it is art, including the police, or else they would have listened to you in the first place."

"Then why the fuck are you here?"

He raised his hands in defeat and said, "Hey, I agree with you—the more I look at that picture, the more I think it could be Julie, and she looks…" Scott hesitated and shook his head. "I don't think anyone could do that to themselves in the name of art, but it is still a felony we're planning to commit. I just needed to reassure myself. I'm sorry."

His words struck me like a spear through the heart, and I had to lean against the desk to prevent myself from slumping to the ground.

Deep down inside, I had still tried to convince myself my assumptions were wrong, that it couldn't be you, but my heart had known better. In the times we had spent together, I had memorized every curve of your body, the way you moved, how the light bounced off your skin. None of this reflected from that first picture, but the birthmark and that scar had told me what I needed to know. It wasn't so much the confirmation of it being you in that picture, but the revelation of what that bastard had done to you. I had only seen that second picture for the briefest of moments, but that didn't take away the dismay that I felt as my eyes fell upon the image.

I couldn't understand why nobody could see the terror behind those images. Scott had appeared impassive as he watched the picture, and I wondered what he saw in them, but I couldn't make myself ask the question. All I knew then was that every bone in my body, every organ, every muscle, every cell needed to get inside that house.

"Then…" I said and hesitated, "there isn't anything left to do except…" Again, I hesitated to voice my thoughts. Scott glanced my way as he rolled the chair to the desk. He must have known what I was thinking. We needed to get inside that house.

"If your observations pan out and from what I've seen these past two days," Scott said, "then we have a pretty wide window to get things done, but you have to be aware of the consequences, and you can't freak out as you just did."

I nodded, unable to answer. It wasn't just the fact that the breaking-and-entering part could get us both arrested that made me uneasy. The thought of what I could find inside made my blood run cold.

Chapter Twelve

Matthew

Scott stood at the window, eying the house across the street with a pair of binoculars. He carried an odd expression on his face as if agitated by something.

I asked, "What is it?"

Scott flinched as if my words had spooked him. He didn't answer my question but instead placed the binoculars on the desk and crossed the room. He sat down on the couch and blew out a breath. I watched him for a moment as he seemed deep in thought and wondered where his mind had run off to. Then his face turned grim as he looked at me.

"You know that if we do this, we could go to jail," he said. "I mean, you could probably claim temporary insanity, but I will be neck deep in it."

I sucked in a breath and moved over to him. Scott kept his eyes on me as I walked around the small table and sat in the chair across from him.

"Listen," I said, "I know the stakes, and I don't expect—"

"All right," Scott said cutting in. A mischievous smirk formed on his face. "I know what I'm getting into, and I just wanted to be sure you did." He leaned forward and placed a finger on one of the floorplans laid out on the table.

Scott was never the type of man to back down from a fight, especially if he felt it would be the right thing to do. Last night after he had returned from checking the cameras, we'd spent the rest of the evening gathering information—not about our photographer friend, but on the other women in his pictures. None of them seemed to have come forth. A mother claimed her lost daughter to be one of the women but couldn't prove it. Her pictures were even more obscure than yours. In an interview, the woman had told a reporter that she had talked to her daughter the night before a big photo shoot with this particular photographer that would have made her career, but that was the last she had heard of her daughter.

It had never led to any serious investigation into our photographer. The police confirmed that girl had been to one of his shoots, but so had many other models that day. Witnesses had confirmed her leaving with a group of friends, and a family member had backed the photographer's alibi. Apparently, he had spent that time with his brother who was a highly decorated officer in the military.

Your second picture had convinced us that we needed to act. It had also made me feel like an idiot. I could never make myself look at it—too scared of what I would find. Although it confirmed what I feared, I doubted it would have made a difference in finding you sooner.

Within a week of your disappearance, the detective working your case had based on the fact that some of your clothes were missing from our place determined that you had left willingly. That along with the fact that your name popped up in relation to an untimely death and your stay at a mental health facility had helped him draw his conclusions quickly. He'd told me that you had probably "flown the coop," as he had put it.

When I returned in that fifth month after I had discovered those pictures to point them in the direction of the photographer, that detective had pretended that he barely knew me. He had probably still been pissed that I had taken my anger out on him. Eventually, I think he'd taken pity on me and offered to look into it, but after only two days, I'd received a message that my suspect had turned out to be a dead-end and that he even doubted that it was you in that picture.

The girls in the photographs, including the photographer himself, had all lived in different states, and besides me, I didn't think anyone had wanted to connect the dots. Five months hadn't caused the detective to change his mind. He'd stated that, even if it had been you in those pictures —reminding me that there hadn't been any evidence to support that fact, I had to face the fact that the woman I loved had left me in search of a career in modeling.

I hadn't been able to believe the police had come up with a similar explanation as some of my friends; especially the ones you never seemed to connect with had spoken out against your intentions. They'd concluded that you had tried to play me and ran after I had found out who you really were. But how could you have known that I had found out about your mom? And I had always known that you had to work hard for the things you wanted. Those so-called friends judged you without even knowing you. They hadn't known that you not opening up had come from an inability to trust people, that it took time for you to come to know someone, that saying, "Hi," to someone and exchanging small talk wasn't enough for you to expose your inner thoughts.

In truth, even I'd had trouble getting through to you, and it had frustrated me too, but since talking to your mother, it had all become so clear. Having lived through those horrors would have clamped up anyone, but how could I have convinced anyone of that without disclosing your innermost secrets?

The police had talked to those same friends and had heard those same stories, so of course, they had created their own version of events. Out of politeness, the detective had put up with me showing up every week, asking for an update, or listening as I presented some new piece of information, but in the end, he'd refused my calls. That's when I'd decided to go after the photographer myself.

Scott tapped a finger on the floorplan.

I asked, "What are you thinking?" I knew my expression must've seemed eager to him, and I didn't want him to think I'd be reckless in my pursuit of finding you, but I couldn't help it.

Scott took a breath and glanced up at me.

He said, "We go in tomorrow morning after the bastard has left the house."

I nodded absently. *Tomorrow morning— that soon!* It chipped away at some of that eagerness inside me, but I knew I had no choice, and I couldn't let the fear of what I might find inside that house overwhelm me.

"I know it'll be risky, doing this in the light of day, but we don't have much choice," Scott said. "The bastard never leaves after he returns home, but I think the neighborhood will allow it."

"What do you mean—allow it?" I asked. Scott shrugged.

"I mean, look around," he said. "Nothing bad ever happens in a neighborhood like this. We're just going to drive around the back and enter as though we belong. No one will be the wiser."

Then he started to explain. I carefully watched as Scott laid out the plan. We went over it five times until my head started to get weary and I decided to call it a night.

Chapter Thirteen

Matthew

That night turned into an unending nightmare as sleep came in fits, only to be replaced by that image of you haunting my mind. Morning couldn't have come soon enough.

The neighborhood seemed eerily quiet as we drove around the block in our unmarked white van. Scott had rented it for the occasion. He had voiced that if we found Julie that she might be in need of getting to the hospital.

"She'd be more comfortable in a van," he had said. I hadn't debated or questioned his idea.

The sun had barely started its climb across the horizon. It was early, and because it was Sunday, we didn't expect many prying eyes.

Still, I felt nervous when we stopped alongside the brick wall that surrounded the photographer's backyard. About half an hour before, we had both witnessed the man leaving, and after he'd driven off in his Prius, we'd waited for another twenty minutes, sitting inside the van.

I stood on unsteady legs as I waited for Scott to open the gate that would lead us into the yard. Scott worked fast, and he had us inside within a minute. I had hoped it would have made me feel better, standing within the confines of the walls surrounding the yard with the risk of being seen reduced to a minimum, but it didn't.

I decided to focus on the plan and not let myself get distracted. We were on a mission, and this mission was you. The thought of seeing you again in any capacity would be worth it. I kept that thought in the forefront of my mind and followed Scott along the wall until he stopped behind a garden shed and kneeled. Trees and the shed had obscured my vision of the house, and as I kneeled next to Scott, I caught my first glimpse of the building not viewed through the lens of a camera.

My heart sank to my stomach. I couldn't explain the reason. Nothing seemed out of the ordinary. A well-maintained yard, trimmed bushes, and grass led up to a porch that gave access to the backdoor, and at the far right corner sat another door that would lead us to the basement of the house. Sand-colored walls complemented the white-painted high-framed windows of the house. But something didn't sit right. A heaviness fell over me, something I couldn't explain, the feeling of pure dread that washed over me the moment I lay eyes upon the house. Maybe the windows obscured by the black curtains had something to do with it, or maybe the way the lights bounced off those windows, but something added to the uneasiness growing inside my gut.

Scott shifted to face me, with squinted eyes and a curious look. *Had he sensed the same?* He shuddered as if a sudden cold breeze had caught the back of his neck. The air was brisk, but we were dressed in warm fleece jackets that snugged tightly around our bodies.

"What?" I asked in a whisper. Scott shook his head and said,

"It's nothing. Just remember the plan and walk as if we belong." Then he got to his feet and started across the lawn. Without hesitation, I followed him. Somehow Scott's presence gave me courage—the courage I needed if I wanted to find you.

Walking behind Scott, I could see the bulge underneath his fleece where his weapon sat concealed. I carried my own Glock with forty-five auto round stopping power equipped with a silencer in the same place. Scott had mentioned using a silencer so that if he had to use it, the weapon wouldn't arouse any neighbors. He hadn't intended on me carrying a gun. It seemed he didn't trust me with it without the proper training, but I had taken one from Scott's bag, along with a fitting silencer, without him knowing. The weapon felt uncomfortable, tucked into the back of my jeans. The fact that I had never fired a gun in my life might have had something to do with it, although it seemed easy enough on TV. I glanced around at the neighboring buildings but didn't expect anyone would be able to see our concealed weapons. Seeing the closed curtains at the few windows in sight, I suspected no one would even see the two of us walking across this lawn. As my gaze returned to the statuesque building, it seemed as if the air shifted.

I felt a weight press down on me as we neared the porch. It felt as if something tried to push me into the ground or as if the magnetic force keeping us grounded had decided to suck us underneath the earth. By the time I reached the basement door, I felt sick, ready to throw up, but managed to hold it together.

I pretended it to be nerves and not the fear of what I would find inside. I started repeating the plan inside my head again. Scott had hammered it into my brain. Not so much the plan, which seemed simple enough, get in—get out, but every detail of the house itself. The location of every room, every door, and every window sat carved inside my brain. If anything went wrong, the first rule was to get out.

My heart pounded inside my chest as I

stood at Scott's side while he fiddled with the lock. Breaking into a person's house wasn't something I usually did. In my line of work as an editor for a flashy magazine, these types of things didn't fit into the job description, although sometimes it made me feel like a voyeur because all I had to do all day was to sit behind a desk and look at pictures to find places for them on the empty pages. Now I felt like a common criminal. However, I knew our cause to be just and even if I had to spend time in jail, it would be worth the chance to save you.

The lock clicked, and Scott eased the door open. He used a flashlight to take a quick glance around and, as he found it safe, pulled me inside.

Closing the door bathed us in darkness. I turned around to place my hand on the window and felt it covered by a black foil. That would explain the darkness. Somehow it felt as if it were too dark. I didn't know whether anything being too dark existed, but it came along with that eerie feeling I had felt walking toward the house.

The beam of Scott's flashlight cut a path through the layers of black to reveal a staircase. The steps went down at a steep angle, and it had been a good thing that I had stopped when I did, because falling down that thing would have surely broken my neck.

I peeked over Scott's shoulder to get a better look, but it seemed as if the flashlight couldn't reach the bottom.

Scott glanced up and shrugged. Then he pulled the gun from under his fleece and took the first steps down. The wooden steps cracked underneath our boots to the chorus of our moving feet. The sound bounced off the concrete walls of the narrow staircase and reverberated back to us.

With every step I took, I felt my breathing getting heavier along with the weight pressing down on me. This felt worse than it had out in the backyard. My heart rate elevated as if it played an extra layer to the drumbeat of the house. I could barely see Scott walking in front of me, even though he carried the flashlight, and I wished I had brought my own.

Scott stopped as we reached the bottom of the stairs, and his flashlight cast a tight beam down the narrow corridor. For a moment I feared we had gotten ourselves stuck in a concrete box, but then his light stopped on a metal door at the end of the hall. Scott stepped forward, and I followed until he turned and pointed his light at me.

The light hit my face, and I lifted my hand to shield my eyes.

"What?" I asked, annoyed, but kept my voice at a whisper.

"Are you all right?" he asked, moving his flashlight over me.

"Fine, why?"

"Because you're breathing like an ox," he replied.

I hadn't noticed, but once Scott had said it, I realized I might have been on the verge of hyperventilating.

"Take a breath," he said, whispering back. "It's just an empty house."

Taking Scott's advice, I took a deep breath, nodded, and then gestured to the door.

I asked, "Should we try it?"

Scott let his flashlight slide along the unpainted concrete as he inspected the door.

"There should be an entry up on the left that should lead us into the kitchen," he said as he started to walk.

The light fought a way through the dark until it came across what looked like a gaping hole. Sure enough, the hole formed into a door-shaped entryway, and Scott showed his light up a set of stairs.

"I'm still kind of hazy about why we're not using the back door to get us into the kitchen," I said in a whisper. "Why are we down here?"

Scott turned, shining the beam from his flashlight right in my face, blinding me for a second. As I grunted my discomfort, he redirected his light and pointed it at the door at the end of the hall.

"I noticed it on the floorplan," he said as he started toward it. He hesitated before he added, "I mean...if you're hiding something."

He didn't clarify, but I knew what he meant. A dark basement would be a good place to do the things you needed to keep away from prying eyes.

I came up behind him and caught a whiff of a strange odor I couldn't place. The foul scent made me shudder, and I knew I had smelled it before, but I had somehow lost the memory.

"What is that?" I asked, placing a hand over my nose and mouth.

"I think it's coming from over there," he said. Passing the stairs that led up to the kitchen, Scott moved closer to the door at the end of the hall. The light from his flashlight flickered once, then twice, as if its batteries had drained.

"This thing is brand-new," he mumbled under his breath as he shook the metal rod.

As I followed him, I felt that weight press down on me again. This time, it wasn't just a feeling that grabbed me. As we stepped closer to the door, the light coming from the flashlight dimmed. I knew it had to be my imagination, but it seemed as if something rejected the light, sucking it up as some black hole in space might have done.

"What the hell," Scott exclaimed. Still, being the soldier he was, he kept going until he reached the door.

Heart pounding, I followed. Everything inside me screamed to turn around, but then Scott had the light, and I felt the urge to stay close. The powerful beam of the flashlight had reduced to a mere trickle of light, bouncing off the metal door.

"This is weird," Scott said as he reached for the nob.

"I'm not sure about this," I said as Scott's hand started to turn. The weight pressing down on me seemed to feed on the fear running from my pores, and this time, I felt overly aware of my heavy breathing.

The lock clicked, and Scott swung the door open.

Chapter Fourteen

Julie

Noises. There were noises. I could hear them, but I couldn't place them. It wasn't the house speaking to me—I was sure of it. I knew its language, although I wished I didn't, and those weren't that. I hadn't heard the rattle of the keys or the click of the lock followed by the opening of the door.

Starting to doubt myself, I wondered if I had fallen asleep. *Had I missed the noises accompanied by the door? Had he returned? Had he deviated from his routine?* I gripped my arms tighter around my body.

Fear took over, and my nerves rattled. *Had I missed him coming home?* I glanced at the light entering through the window. The sun hadn't even found its way to its highest point. Then I realized light still poured inside the room. As had become my routine, I had removed the foil that morning after I had heard him leave.

I had to cover the window, but my hands trembled so much I feared I'd tear the foil.

What would happen if he entered and found me sitting on the toilet with access to the outside world? What would it do to me if he found me ignoring his orders? What would happen to me?

I couldn't fathom the thoughts—I couldn't move, but I knew I needed to cover the window and hide the light. I wetted my thumb using my tongue and smeared saliva across the glass. My shaky fingers reached for the foil, trying to ease it back into place. The foil ripped in places as I fumbled with the thin material. Gradually the light started to disappear. My fingers pressed on the glass, moving the foil into place.

I breathed a little easier as darkness surrounded me again. In the dark, it seemed as if I had done a good-enough job, and I didn't think he would notice as long as he didn't turn on the light. With the lights out, he wouldn't be able to see the cracks in the foil anyway.

I forced my hands from the glass. That was as good as I would get it. I drew in a breath, hoping it would keep me from throwing up. As I climbed to my feet, I paused and listened. The house seemed quiet again, but the drumming of my heart seemed to overrule my hearing. My legs felt as if they had turned to Jell-O, and they trembled as I shifted to my good leg to carry the weight of my body. Although the incident with the hammer seemed as if it had happened ages ago, my knee still hurt as if it had happened yesterday.

I raised my foot to lift it inside the bathtub as the sound of footsteps coming from downstairs shocked me. Frantic footsteps in an area of the house where I wasn't used to hearing them reached my ears through the door. For all I had been able to hear, he only seemed to use the one room downstairs, the one underneath this bathroom, the one connecting to the stairs that would lead up here. Except for the noises of the house as it spoke to me in its own language, I had never heard sounds coming from other areas, and certainly had I never heard sounds this frantic.

Somewhere inside a door slammed shut, and then I heard the pounding of feet running down the hall downstairs. Fear wrapped around me, and I couldn't breathe. *He had returned. He must have.*

I couldn't move. Fear had frozen me in place. He had never acted this erratically, and I didn't want to imagine what could have set him into this state. *What this would mean for me.*

A step on the stairs cracked loudly. Feet pounded, racing upstairs, skipping every other step. I had lost count, but he was on his way. I scrambled backward and stumbled over the edge of the tub. I fell, landing hard on my elbow inside the metal tub. I couldn't help the groan that escaped my mouth, but bit my lip and managed not to cry out.

Heavy boots stopped on the landing and then seemed to turn into a circle as if searching for something. *Had he gone mad?*

I crawled into the corner of my tub, curling up into the tiniest ball I'd ever managed. My hands shook so hard that it was hard to hang on to my legs as I pulled them tighter to my chest.

I squeezed my eyes shut, dreading the moment he would open that door. *What would he do to me?* I couldn't bear to spend another second in that chair. *He couldn't do that to me.* I hadn't done anything wrong, not this time, but then I remembered the torn foil covering the window, and I wanted to scream. *Why had I done that? Why had I felt this desperate need for some connection to the outside world? What would that need cost me?* He would come for me, and I would finally get what I deserved.

Tears ran down my cheeks as I tried to breathe. The moment the voice called out it seemed as if the world stopped.

Chapter Fifteen

Matthew

"Julie!" I called out. It seemed ridiculous. There had been no sign, no indication that you might be here, that you were still alive, but I felt it so strongly. *You had to be here.* I just knew it. I called your name out again as I circled the landing holding the gun out in front of me.

My heart felt as if it wanted to rip a hole in my chest. *Had that just happened? Had that been real?* Recapturing what had happened, I tried to retrace my steps. Scott had opened the door. Scott, Scott, my mind kept repeating his name. *Scott, where had he gone?*

I stopped, turning, and pointed the gun at a door down the hall. For a moment, the weight lifted, the weight that had pressed down on me from the moment I had stepped onto this property, just for a fraction of a second before the memories came rushing down on me.

Scott had opened the metal door and then…Screams…Scott had screamed as the darkness had come. The darkness had engulfed him as his flashlight had died, darkness wrapping around him like a blanket, swallowing him whole. The shock of Scott's unearthly screams threw me back, and I had crashed to the ground.

Pushing up, I'd found myself surrounded by darkness. The light Scott had carried had vanished. I'd flung my arms out into the dark, feeling its density, but hadn't been able to find Scott. His screams had bounced off the concrete in every direction. The dread coming from his voice had torn at me as if it could peel the skin and rip the flesh from my bones. It had come from all around me. My head had swirled around, but only black had surrounded me—crushing me. I hadn't been able to see my hands in front of my eyes.

"Scott!" I'd shouted. "Scott, please…" I'd wanted to reach out to him, wanted to help, but he'd kept screaming into the void, and I hadn't been able to find him.

"Please, Scott," I had said aloud as I'd pleaded with him, "talk to me. What's happening?" My mind hadn't been able to fathom what was happening, my eyes hadn't been able to see, and Scott's pained voice had filled my ears.

Then Scott's voice had muted as if someone had shoved a sock in his mouth. *Could someone have been down here with us and had they grabbed Scott?* I'd shouted his name and tried to follow the muffled sounds. It couldn't have been the photographer; we had both watched him leave. Finding the wall, I had struggled to my feet and used it to find my way in pursuit of Scott. Fear had wrapped around me as if the darkness surrounding me had been made of it. I'd pushed forward, but it had been as if my legs moved through mud.

A loud clank of metal against stone had reverberated inside the narrow space, and I'd had to cover my ears to protect them from the sound. As I'd released my ears, the muffled screams had stopped.

Taking several more steps, I had come to a sudden halt as I'd walked into the door. At least I'd thought it to be the door. My hands had slid over the metal, but I hadn't been able to find the door handle. Frantically, my hands had searched the door.

"Scott!" I'd shouted. "Scott, talk to me!" My fists had pounded on what I'd thought to be the door, but it had been as if they'd hit concrete. It hadn't sounded as if there had been a hollow space behind it.

My heart had hammered inside my chest as I'd tried to catch my breath, but I hadn't seemed to be able to get air into my lungs. As before, my breathing had come close to hyperventilating, and I'd fallen to my knees.

"Breathe, breathe," I'd chanted in a whisper to myself—reminding me of the words spoken by Scott. Just an empty house, but had it been? *What if I'd been wrong and someone else lived here?* Someone must have overpowered Scott, but where were they? This might just be a person living here, urged to defend their home. *What if I'd been wrong about everything and that someone was calling the cops right now? If you weren't here and I got myself arrested, then how would I ever be able to find you?*

Around me, I'd felt the dreaded darkness

take hold of me as doubt started to reel me in. I had been able to feel it press down on me as if hands had grabbed my throat and wanted to squeeze the air out of me. I shook my head. No, I couldn't be wrong about this. If I was wrong, then that meant you wouldn't be here. This didn't make any sense. I'd had to get out of here, and I had climbed to my feet. My gut clenched at the thought of leaving Scott behind, but there wasn't anything else I could do. Feeling my way along the walls, I'd run. I'd run until I'd found that hole in the wall with the steps leading up, and I'd suddenly found myself thinking of you.

I forced Scott to the back of my mind as I'd run up the stairs. Fleeing from the depths of the house, I'd exited the staircase and run into something hard. I had bent over colliding with a table hidden in the dark. Metal had clanged as it had fallen from the table onto the ground—the sounds of pots and pans connecting with the tiled floor. I must have found the kitchen Scott had mentioned. Finding my balance, I'd peered into the darkness and noticed a shred of light.

I'd run to it and had found a hall. A door stood in the wall on my left. Without thinking, I'd thrown my weight into it, slamming my shoulder against its solid surface. Pain had seared through my shoulder as it had connected with the door without success. I'd tried again, but the door hadn't budged. As my fists had pounded on the old wood, I'd shouted your name but had received no reply.

My heart raced as my eyes scanned the rest of the hall and found another door on the right. This time, I rammed my other shoulder into the door. The wood cracked, and the door swung open.

Inside revealed a narrow living room with basic-looking furniture. A light coming from a screen turned from my field of vision lit the room in an eerie green glow, but otherwise, the room sat empty.

A small window over the solid wooden front door allowed a sliver of sunlight to find its way inside the house at the end of the hall as I ran past a series of black-and-white photographs barely visible in the dim light. Without looking at them, I knew what images they held, but I couldn't stop to think about them. At the front door, I turned and bolted up the stairs. I didn't even stop to check if the door would open because I could only think of you. Scott and what had happened to him lingered at the back of my mind along with the fact that someone else might be inside the house with me, but at that point, I couldn't think straight. I had to find you.

That was how I had gotten myself up here, but what had happened? Unable to think, I followed that sensation that momentarily overtook my senses. You hid in that sensation, and I followed it to the door down the hall.

I found a switch and clicked on a light. The sudden brightness of it hurt my eyes. Squinting, I found the locks keeping the door in place, and I started to unlatch them; fortunately, no keys were needed. From behind the door, I heard the tiniest whimper that made my heart skip a beat. *Could it be true? Could this be you?*

Somehow, my entire being had already made the decision it had to be you, and I jerked the door open.

Darkness greeted me inside the room, along with a smell similar to what I had encountered in that narrow corridor down in the basement, and it triggered my memory.

I had smelled it before, during a photo shoot no less. Some hotshot wannabe photographer had come up with the idea to place his models on the stainless steel tables of a morgue. It had been the pathologist who explained how over four hundred volatile, organic compounds produced by bacteria would break down the tissue in the body into gasses and salts.

I shuddered at the thought as I inhaled the sickly sweet smell of death. The entire house seemed intoxicated by it. *How had I not recognized it before? Why hadn't Scott mention it?*

A soft whimper reached me through my

haze of thoughts, and I snapped out of it. I squinted as I tried to adjust my eyes to the light from the hall as it penetrated the darkness of a bathroom, and I noticed the dark shape inside the tub. It took me a moment to recognize the balled-up features of a human being.

My heart stopped as I took a step. Emotions clashed inside me, as my mind didn't know whether to feel joy or fear. *Had I finally found you?*

I fell to my knees in front of the tub and whispered your name.

"Julie."

"No, no, no..." Your quivering voice spoke in a barely audible tone. "Please... don't hurt me."

My heart sank into the pit of my stomach and reached out a shaking hand to touch you.

"Julie," I whispered, "baby, it's okay, it's me." I wanted to comfort you, but it seemed as if you didn't even recognize my voice. You wouldn't look up as your body trembled. I touched your shoulder, and you winced.

"Please, Julie..." I said and hesitated. Then I tentatively cupped your cheek and forced you to face me. Your entire body trembled as you kept your eyes closed shut, and I leaned over so I could press my forehead to yours. You violently shook your head and pulled away from my touch.

"Julie, my love," I said, "it's me."

You didn't seem to recognize my voice, and I begged you to open your eyes. As if your lids opened for the first time, slowly you revealed your eyes. I kept talking to you— letting you hear my voice. You had to recognize my voice. Then you blinked, and in the faint light coming from the hallway, I could see your eyes widen.

"Matthew," you said. Your voice sounded broken and unused as if you hadn't spoken the entire six months you'd been gone.

I refused to look around the bathroom that someone had turned into your tomb. I couldn't allow the distraction by the thoughts of anguish you must have felt, the fear, the pain, and the loneliness—they would have overwhelmed me. I shook the thought from my mind. You weren't alone anymore. You had me, and I had to get you out of this house.

Chapter Sixteen

Julie

I heard your voice, but that couldn't be. *You weren't here.* No one was here except for him and me. I had never heard him speak words in kindness. I had barely heard him speak at all. Yet these words spoken in kindness revealed a spark of hope. *Could this be real? Had you come for me?* That spark of hope loosened the muscles in my face, and I peered through the slits of my half-opened lids.

The face so close to mine was one I had only thought to see in dreams again, those handfuls of dreams that had made a life in this darkness bearable. I reached a hand up to touch that face. *Your face.* As I pricked my fingers on the stubble on your cheeks, it finally became reality. *You were here. You were actually here.*

I sat up and wrapped my arms around your neck. You pulled me close, which left the edge of the bathtub a cold reminder on my bare skin where my shirt failed to cover my stomach. It didn't matter. Soon this would be over—another bad memory, ready to be locked away in a drawer in the depths I knew my mind could reach. Hiding my past from everyone as well as myself had become my way of life.

Tears ran down my cheeks as I felt my heart pound inside my chest, eager to melt with yours.

I wasn't ready to let you go as you pushed me at arms' length, but my body was weak, and you were so strong. As your eyes took me in, I caught the pained expression on your face and felt a misplaced sense of shame about all that I must have put you through.

Then your features changed. The corner of your mouth angled up, and I could see the relief in your eyes. Your strong arms helped me step out of the bathtub, and I wrapped my arms around you.

It was as if the fear had left me. That even being inside this room, inside this house that would spend its time talking to me through the cracks and ticks of the old wood, would be fine for as long as you were with me. I wanted to hold on to that feeling and never let you go, but I should have known a feeling like that had to be fleeting, although I hadn't expected it to be ripped from my core by the rattle of keys.

Something inside the house shifted as I heard the front door lock click shut. The light in the hall outside the bathroom seemed to dim, but it must have been a trick of the eyes. A dark, heavy weight leaned down on my shoulders, and as a chill ran down my body, I froze. I didn't know whether you had heard the noise, but you must have felt the renewed tension in my body.

I looked up to find your eyes, and I could see the concern filling them. You thought it was me. You hadn't heard, and I struggled to open my mouth.

I said, "He's...here." The sounds were hoarse, but the fear rolling off my voice was unmistakable. My hand trembled as I pointed past the door and in the direction of the staircase. Your head shifted to follow my line of sight as the first step of the staircase creaked.

Chapter Seventeen

Matthew

The weight of fear fell down on the both of us, and I could feel your body tense up in my arms. Your hand shook as hard as my heart thumped against my chest. Another crack reverberated up the stairs and then another. Slow, steady footsteps, carefully placed on each step, seemed unable to create the sound that followed as the weight pressed down on the old wooden stairs. A loud crack followed by silence...crack. As if the wood spoke in its own voice.

I stepped in front of you to protect you with my body and tightened my grip on the gun's handle. The metal clicked as my thumb switched off the safety. Crack...

You held on to me as I eased us forward, gun raised. I squeezed your hand, hoping to reassure you, but knew it to be a vain attempt. Fear was a hard thing to see in a person's eyes, and I saw it in yours. I didn't need to know the details of how much you'd suffered. It had broken something inside you, and it showed. Although your boney features and gaunt face told me your body had taken the brunt force of it, I knew your mind must have had to endure much worse. Still, as you stood there by my side, I knew that if I managed to get you out of here, you would survive this. Survive as you had before. Except this time, it would be up to me to get you past the threshold.

The wooden steps stopped cracking. From my memory of the layout of this house, I knew there were several rooms on this floor, but none of them led to a way out. Our only chance was to escape the photographer and flee through the front or back door. Breaking the window inside the bathroom wasn't an option. It wouldn't be safe to jump, especially not with Julie.

I drew in a breath. I had seen the man, and although the pictures I had found online were grainy and often obscured. For someone so infamous in the art world, the man had done his work to keep his appearance hidden. He had kept a low profile, but from what I had seen of him, he looked gangly to me. With my weekly workout at the gym and daily rowing on the river, I had built up a fit and capable body that should be able to take him down. That and the fact that I was armed. Still, I had no way of knowing whether he was armed.

A door opened and shut at the end of the hall. You squeezed my hand, and I chanced a quick glance at you in an attempt to reassure you before my gaze returned to the door. You kept your face hidden in the shadows as your body hid behind mine. You didn't voice your thoughts, but I figured them to be the same as mine. *We were about to confront the man that had done this to you.*

Chapter Eighteen

Julie

I clung to your body as you took a step. He had returned and had come upstairs. He never came upstairs immediately. He had always, always entered the room on the left of the front door first—always. My mind raced as I tried to pull up the sounds embedded in my memories. *Had he ever used one of the other rooms?* I couldn't remember. Except for the room he had brought me to if he needed me to sit in the chair, I had never heard him enter another room. He had deviated from his routine. He was waiting for us. He had seen the light; he knew the door was open. *Oh God, what would he to us? What would he do to you?*

I needed to warn you, needed to let you know that this wasn't just a man. I had felt his strength, had seen his form, and although I would never doubt your capabilities, but even with the gun in your hand, I couldn't dampen the fear raging through my body. As you crossed the threshold into the light of the hall, I pulled at your fleece jacket, but I couldn't make a sound. As if someone had stolen my vocal cords, my throat wouldn't let me speak.

The light flickered in the hallway, and as I looked around, more and more shadows climbed the walls. It was as if something pulled at the light in an attempt to bathe us in darkness.

You stopped and a cold chill ran down my spine. My breath caught in my throat and nearly choked me. Something heavy pressed down on me as if it wanted to squash me into the cracks between the floorboards underneath my feet. The light flickered again and reduced to something barely resembling the flame of a candle. I glanced over your shoulder and screamed.

Chapter Nineteen

Matthew

Your screams tore at my heart. I couldn't stand the pain and fear that came from your voice, but then I had to face my own fears.

I stumbled backward, forcing you to retreat into the room that had become your personal hell. I had no choice as my eyes fell on the man standing before me. *A man…hell, was it a man?* A figure cloaked in darkness as if he rejected the light stood mere feet from me, but I recognized some of the features of the gangly photographer.

He hadn't been there a second ago. It was as if I had blinked, and he had appeared —waiting for us, as if he had known we would be here.

You pulled at my jacket, and I took another step back while he just stood there. I couldn't see all of his face, as it sat obscured by a hood. As my eyes adjusted and penetrated his shroud of darkness, he didn't seem to be much of a man. My boot scraped the threshold to the bathroom, and I almost tripped.

Around us, wood cracked and creaked as if someone else resided inside the house. I wanted to wrap my arms around you but was afraid to point the gun in any other direction than our assailant.

I glanced down to see you tucked into my side, hiding your face in my jacket. At that moment, his voice opened up.

"You dare to come here and take what is mine."

Chapter Twenty

Julie

The light inside the hallway went out just as you raised your hand to shoot. They weren't the ear-piercing blasts I would have expected that echoed inside the room as the gun fired several shots. They sounded like muffled hisses but didn't seem to have any effect. He came at us with the ferociousness of a venomous snake and the strength of a bull as he slammed into us. He ripped us apart, and I felt your hand slip from my grasp. The force of the blow sent me tumbling down onto the edge of the bathtub, but I managed to keep myself from falling in. I landed on my butt next to the tub.

With the light in the hall out, the darkness wrapped around me, pressing me down as I cowered next to the tub and clutched my legs to my chest. The house seemed to have come to life, and it shook with the effort. These weren't the eerie sounds I had to listen to, lying cold and alone in that bathtub. This felt as if a level-five tornado had landed dead center inside the house, tearing the room apart inch by inch. Underneath my bare feet, I felt the tiles crack into a million pieces. I heard wood snap like twigs as when walking around in a forest but then multiplied by a hundred. If I had taken a second to think about it, I might have realized that my mind had conjured up all these sensations that seemed so unreal to begin with, but there wasn't time to think—I couldn't think.

You grunted with effort from what sounded like a struggle, but I couldn't see. A loud clank of metal on metal sounded as something fell into the tub. You called out, but the words made no sense to me. My hands covered my ears. I was afraid to listen, to hear your screams in pain, but words formed between those screams. You wanted me to hear what you had to say. I still didn't want to, but I knew that soon I might never hear words again, and I wanted the last ones to be yours.

I released my ears, and grabbed the edge of the tub. The wind struck my face along with the knife-sharp pieces of tiles that had come loose from the broken walls. I didn't understand what was happening. *This couldn't be real. Had my mind finally forsaken me?* Too scared to open my eyes, it seemed that my other senses had either left me or tried to trick me. Trapped behind the darkness of my eyelids, I heard you yell a single phrase, *"Gun!"*

It took me a moment to realize what you wanted to say, but then I remembered the loud clank and something falling into the bathtub. You needed help, and I was the only one who could give it. Taking a shuddering breath and knowing it to be fruitless, I opened my eyes. In the unchanging darkness, I reached into the tub, feeling around for the hunk of metal.

Chapter Twenty-One

Matthew

As the lights had gone out, I had blindly fired several shots in the hope one would take him out, but he kept coming at me. Stumbling backward, he had forced me to the ground and pinned me against the wall between the bathtub and the toilet. As he struggled to keep me down with his full weight on top of me. I flung my fist at him and felt it connect, but it seemed the photographer was a scrappy fellow. As I struggled to get a fix on the man, I wanted to curse myself for not acting accordingly and standing frozen inside that bathroom instead of bolting for the stairs.

One of the man's fists struck my shoulder instead of my face as he fought blind, and I shouted your name. I needed you to listen to me, but you seemed to have disappeared. The gun had fallen from my hands, and I had heard it drop into the tub. There would be no way for me to reach it. It didn't matter; I had claimed the photographer's focus. My body pressed into the wall, and I had trouble breathing. All I wanted was a fair chance and for you to get out. I needed you to be safe. My legs kicked out but struck nothing. Pressure pushed against my chest, and I feared my ribs would start breaking one by one. The fact that this gangly man had me pinned on my back pissed me off and fueled the rage pumping through my veins, but I had his focus. As I fought to regain the upper hand, I hoped, prayed, that you had already fled the room or that if you hadn't that my voice would reach your mind, that you realized it was me saying them because I needed you to be safe. I drew in a breath and screamed for you to *run!*

Chapter Twenty-Two

Julie

The gun felt warm in my cold hand as I tried to get to my feet. My battered knee screamed in pain as I forgot to shift my weight. The room that had become my world these past months had shifted. I couldn't fathom the change. *Was this for real, or had my mind fabricated it?* Wind raged around me, tugging at my flimsy clothes and pushing my body off-balance. My legs were too fragile, unused, and too unstable, and I fell to my knees. More pain shot up my legs, but nothing felt more agonizing than hearing you suffer.

Peering into the darkness, I heard your struggle. Boots scuffled on the tiles and slammed into the metal tub. You seemed in pain as your voice repeated the word *gun*.

I couldn't listen anymore. I had to act, just as I had all those years ago. *You needed me to act, but how could I?*

Your body fought with something impervious to bullets somewhere in the corner of this room. You had shot at him at close range, and the bullets had done nothing to stop his attack. The light in the hallway had gone out, and shooting the man would be hard enough even without being able to see him, but what if the bullets hit you? I would die if you got hurt because of me.

The metal of the gun felt heavy as I raised it, and I had trouble holding it steady. Surrounded by darkness, the images inside my mind threatened to run me over. My father's vacant eyes stared back at me as I tried to control my breathing. I couldn't shake the image that had haunted me for years.

The sound of the struggle along with the house that seemed to vent its rage pulled me out of my haze. I couldn't let that image of my father turn into you; I wouldn't. I rested my elbow on the edge of the tub and added my other hand to raise the gun higher. Nothing could force me to hurt you, but you were already hurt. You were dying, and I took the shot.

The blackened glass shattered as two bullets struck the window. Light poured into the room and stung at my eyes. Tears blurred my vision, masking the facts before my eyes. I gasped at the unfolding dark shadow that had taken hold of you. For a moment, all I could see was you, surrounded by a black, ghostly mass, a dark entity that didn't belong in this world. I struggled to accept the images fed to my mind through hazy eyes. *This could not be real. This had to be a trick of some kind.* I forced myself to think, but trying to rationalize the situation didn't make the fear disappear.

Hidden from my sight, I heard the sound of thrown punches from behind the bathtub followed by your voice.

You said, "Get the hell off me, you fucking psychopath." Then a body fell backward with a grunt and hit the ground in front of me. Before I could react, he pulled my feet out from under me, and I crashed to the ground. Hands wrapped around me, trying to get a hold of me. In a panic, I flailed my arms in an attempt to ward him off and pointed the gun at him. He startled me as he reached for the gun in my hand and I failed to pull the trigger. As he tightened his hold on me, I lost my grip, and the gun fell to the ground. One of his arms held me in a chokehold while the other tried to reach for the weapon.

He spun me around so I had to face the light coming from the window. I squinted against the harsh brightness until a shadow fell over me. Without being able to see and with only hope to guide me in this struggle, I reached for the weapon before he could get to it and threw the gun in the direction of the shadow, praying it was you blocking the sunlight.

Nothing seemed to register as it should, as if my senses had gone into overdrive. Sounds around me exploded. Something shiny reflected the light and blinded me before I felt the pain. A force pushed me to a side, and my head connected with what I assumed to be the bathtub. Unable to conceive the sensory overload trying to consume me, I felt hands slide up my arms and up my neck. His boney face appeared inches from mine as his hands tightened around my throat. I gasped, trying to suck in air. A sliver of light accentuated his hollow cheeks and pale skin. Blood-filled eyes nearly bulged from his skull and spit flew from his mouth as he said, "How?"

"How?" he repeated the words in a high-pitched shriek as he shook my whole body. His mouth lifted into a sneer contorting his face into something unnatural. Lips pulled from snarling teeth, and his eyes grew even wider. I blinked in an attempt to refocus, hoping it would aid my mind to make sense of what was happening.

His hands pulled me forward but released me as I tried to jerk free. My head snapped back and again connected with the cold metal of the bathtub.

Pain, pain, pain was all I could feel, see, and hear. I made my body small, pulling my legs to my chest as I had always done as he had entered the room. But now he wasn't here to pick up a tray.

Forcing my eyelids to open a crack, I

saw his black mass thrash around us. The wind rushed in through the window along with the light and collided with the swirl of darkness. Like weather fronts pressing down on each other, the wind increased and the small tornado continued to tear the room apart.

My hair whipped at my face. Plaster rained down on me as the wind ripped the tiles from the wall and sucked them into the twister's grasp. The house shook, and I feared it might crumple into a heap of brick and old wood along with us inside. All sorts of things clattered to the ground, but I refused to look. I couldn't make sense of these things as I fought a reality inside my head that couldn't be real.

Another muffled hiss seemed to shift the atmosphere inside the room again, but as the winds died down, I could still hear the screaming. My mind couldn't take it anymore. Screams, screams were all I heard until I felt a hand on my shoulder. I sucked in a breath as I flinched in fear, jerking my body from its grasp. My sudden rush of air intake made me realize the screaming had come from me.

"It's okay. I'm here," your soothing voice spoke, but I refused to trust in it. My fingers clawed at the tiles on the floor, pressing my body into a tighter ball, deeper into the nook between the bath and the wall. I wanted to disappear. I couldn't be here anymore.

Your voice repeated the words, and I tried to listen to them. I wanted them to be true, but how could they? There couldn't be any merit to those words. Wasn't that what *he* had told me this entire time—that I deserved this. *Was this his newest form of torture, making me believe you had come for me?*

A soft prickle grazed my knuckles followed by a kiss. I froze, unable to place the gesture, but it didn't stop the shivers running up and down my body as a sliver of hope fluttered in my stomach.

"Please, baby," your voice spoke. "Please come back to me, we have to go."

I couldn't stop hearing your voice.

"Please just open your eyes."

A brisk gust of wind toyed with my hair and brought along the crisp smell of spring. Birds chirping reached my ears and drilled into my mind. I hadn't heard a bird or breathed fresh air in months. Your voice followed the chirps and finally reached me.

"You're going to be okay. I promise," you said in a whisper near my ear.

Easing my eyes open, I barely noticed the bathroom around me or the light as it filtered in through the broken window. All I could focus on was you.

Sweat matted your dark, wavy hair, and this time, it wasn't meant as a deliberate hairstyle. It all seemed so bright, as if the light exploded around me. Your eyes held mine as they adjusted to the sunlight filtering in, and I raised a hand to caress the stubble on your cheek. *You were real.* As the reality of it finally sank in, I greedily wrapped my arms around you. You picked me up off the floor and carried me in your strong arms. As you stepped from the bathroom into the hall, your body shifted.

Gripping my arms tighter around your

neck, I glanced over your shoulder. The body of a thin man lay on the floor of the hall. His mouth stood open, and it stressed the sharp features in his face. His eyes sat closed, but not the hole oozing blood from his head. *Was this for real? Was this who had kept me here all this time—this man?* My memories of the man revealed a different image. An image of a massive figure with broad shoulders and apparent strength. My eyes glanced in the direction of the devastation inside the bathroom, but there was no devastation to find. Except for the broken window and the bloodied body in the hall, nothing had changed. There weren't any broken tiles or glass or any kind of devastation. *It had all seemed so real.* My mind couldn't make sense of any of this. I didn't recognize the lanky figure lying on the floor. He didn't resemble anything of the large man that had brought me my trays with stale bread and sour milk. As the moment of his hands wrapped around my throat replayed inside my mind, I realized that even his voice hadn't resembled the deep, low-spoken words that had taunted me as I cowered in that bathtub. Maybe I had conjured it all inside my mind, and none of it had been as I had experienced it. Perhaps I had lost it. Along with the realization came the fact that I didn't care. I could live without understanding what I had witnessed inside that room, and I could live without knowing who the dead man lying on the floor was as long as I got out of here alive and had you back in my life. I tightened my grip around your neck.

The steps cracked and creaked but not as loudly as they once had. I closed my eyes as you moved through the house. I refused to look at the place that had once filled my mind with ghostly sounds and scared me awake from the few good dreams I'd had. The old wood moaned under your weight, but I kept my eyes closed even as I felt the warm sunlight on my skin.

You kneeled, and the cold, damp grass tickled my feet as you sat me down. Then you cupped my face with your hands, and only then I dared to open my eyes. Sunlight opened up your face. Your mouth curved into a smile that lighted up your eyes. My lips cracked painfully, but it wouldn't prevent me from smiling at you.

You turned your head and glanced at the house. I followed your gaze and noticed someone sitting on the porch.

Chapter Twenty-Three

Matthew

"Jesus, Scott," I called out as I watched him raise to his feet from where he was sitting on the porch, "what happened?"

I turned to you as I felt your hand grab a fistful of my fleece jacket.

"It's okay," I whispered as I kissed the top of your head. "It's just Scott."

Scott slipped a pair of sunglasses from his pocked and placed them on his nose as he stepped onto the porch.

He said, "Hey Matt. What took you so long?"

Overhead, dark clouds moved in from the east, blocking out the sun and effectively rendering Scott's sunglasses useless. He didn't bother to remove them as a cold breeze created a shiver that started at my neck and ran down my spine. An eerie feeling rose from the pit of my stomach, and my pounding heart shifted into gear.

My head turned at the sound of your whimpers at my side. Tears glazed your eyes, and the blood had drained from your face, making you even paler than before. Your body had frozen in place, holding a tight grip on my arm. Seeing you like this, I felt the weight pressing down on me return. If I hadn't been kneeling in the grass already, I was sure my legs would have buckled.

I glanced back at Scott, unsure of what was happening, and my eyes widened. Scott stood on the edge of the porch, gun raised.

"Tell me," he said in a low, menacing voice, "have you finally figured out why you are here?"

Chapter Twenty-Four

Matthew

Days had passed since I had seen Scott standing on that porch and I still don't seem to fathom the reality of it. My former best friend had been pissed at me for killing the brother I didn't even knew he had, and I fear we might have come to a conclusion of this story.

After he had broken my nose the day before, Scott set off into a conversation as if we were still the friends we once were. He said, "All I wanted was to repay my brother for what had done for me after I came back from the war." Blood still flowed freely from my nose as I started to write, and it showed on the pages of that day.

"I'm not surprised that you don't remember him," he continued. "My brother suffered from severe OCD and his frustrations often led to severe outbursts of anger and violence. Our parents moved him into a facility for special-needs kids after we moved to Seattle and before I met you.

"I must have been eight or nine at the time," he added as an afterthought.

He paced the room as if he were a wild animal imprisoned inside a cage. Wild eyes darted from me to the perfectly spaced pictures hanging on the wall. His brother's masterpieces, he called them. The sight of them made me feel sick to my stomach, and I kept my eyes low so I wouldn't have to face those shocking images.

I shifted uncomfortably in my seat and felt the restraints that kept my feet bound to the chair cut into my skin. This drew his attention back to me, and he stopped pacing.

He said, "You should have seen your face…down there…in that basement." He grinned and couldn't hide the evil that lurked behind his eyes. "I figured I could have some fun with you. It's not as great as the real deal, but those night vision goggles gave a good impression of you scurrying away in the dark."

As if the words triggered some memory, his eyes glanced up at the wall of pictures, and he raised a hand to rub his neck.

"You had to take one of my weapons," he said accusingly, but his voice barely reached a whisper. "I hadn't even heard Travis enter, and because you had been crafty enough to use one of my silencers, I hadn't heard the shots." Scott shook his head in disbelief. "With the front door locked, I wanted to surprise the two of you on the back porch, I wanted to see the expression on your faces after you realized it had been all for nothing, but I guess in retrospect the surprise was mine." As I glanced up at him, his eyes narrowed on me.

"I warned Travis not to intervene, but I should have known he wouldn't be able to leave it alone. I think he might have been a little jealous of you and didn't trust me to stop you from taking Julie."

"Don't expect...me to feel..." I started to say, but had to take a breath before I could finish my sentence, "sorry for that—"

"Don't!" he said, cutting me off. I didn't have the energy left to counter him, so I just shut my mouth and dropped my head, but

Scott wasn't finished yet.

"My little brother couldn't help the way his mind was wired," he said. "He had this primal need to capture the insanity with his camera as it overtook his subjects. It was like a drug to him, but Julie wouldn't give him that satisfaction. He didn't understand what kept her going—frankly, neither did I for the longest time—in the end, it had been that obsession that had gotten him killed."

As if something shifted inside him, his eyes brightened, and he started talking about you.

He said, "We wanted to find out what had kept her relative sanity, and I must admit Travis had even me fascinated with her."

Engaged in his own story, he stepped closer to the table and leaned on it, placing his hands palms down on the top. Although it hurt, I lifted my head to face him. It was the only sign of defiance I had left in me, although I didn't think Scott would recognize it. My mom had been right; those two tours had left him insane. He watched me for a moment before he narrowed his eyes and cocked his head.

He said, "Do you know what happens to a person when you keep them in the dark long enough?" He paused as if waiting for a reply, but I didn't give him one, and he continued.

"It's fascinating to watch the doubts over one's own identity grow by the hour," he said. "You can see their abilities to process information wither away like a leaf trapped underneath a layer of snow. They'd wake up screaming, unable to remember where they were or even who they are."

As he spoke, I could tell the mere thoughts that came with the words exhilarated him. He had enjoyed doing this to all the people displayed in those framed pictures hanging on these walls. It had brought him pleasure to watch them suffer. But I wasn't thinking about the things he had done to all those nameless faces. All I could think about was that he had done this to you and would continue to do so.

"With the help of some sound effects,

insinuations start to build in their heads along with paranoid allusions. It made for some great pictures," he said. "My brother relished immortalizing these transitions with his camera—he lived for it. But this all stopped when I introduced Julie into his life."

My breath caught as he spoke your name. I wanted to lunge for him and wrap my hands around his throat until his eyes popped out of his head. Instead, I felt the restraints dig into my skin. Scott grinned as he watched me squirm.

"Don't...you...say..." I started to say. At least I tried to say it. My words came out ragged and hoarse and I took a breath to finish. "Her...*name!*" I managed to emphasize the last word. All it did was widen the grin on Scott's face as he continued.

"At first, it happened so similarly to the rest of them, but then it came to a halt. As with the others, Julie gave me such pleasures cowering inside that bathroom, and her body reacted perfectly to the brutal diet to add a little drama and texture to the pictures. Everything hinted at my brother's next masterpiece, but then things changed, or should I say, they didn't? We couldn't explain it. While the others had gone stir crazy within a few weeks, Julie had managed to keep her wits—at least to an extent. That's why only two pictures have been released in her series."

I wanted to be strong, to keep my face deprived of emotions, but I couldn't stop the tears running down my cheeks. My left eye was almost swollen shut, and it had leaked fluids ever since he had stopped using my face as his personal punching bag, but I think he could tell that these were real tears. He watched me with fascination as if he had never seen a man cry before, and he leaned in closer. Hell, if I had more strength, I would have tried to head-butt him, but I decided against it. It wouldn't have done me any good, and my head hurt enough as it was. Instead, I watched him pull out a chair and sit across from me.

He said, "And that's why Travis urged

me to involve you. I didn't understand his reasoning and I sort off liked having Julie around, but he thought it might push her over the edge and he would be able to finish his work." He folded his hands and used them to support his chin. He glanced up at the pictures again. "The fact was that I didn't want him to finish his work."

I lifted my head to face him. *What had he meant by that?* Scott held my gaze with a smirk on his face. As if he could read my mind he said, "What I did, I did for my brother, and I would have continued to do so, but he is dead now." He paused as if he could add to the tension already filling the room. "She's mine now."

My head swirled at his admission. My stomach clenched as bile rose in my throat.

"What's wrong Matt," Scott said with a grin. "You look a little pale."

My mind sort of zoned in and out after that. His words had rattled my brain. *What had he planned for you?* I could see him sitting across from me and watched his mouth move, but I didn't feel as if I were there.

Some of his words filtered through about how he would have done anything for his brother. I didn't think Scott to be a person to let anyone tell him what to do, let alone his little brother. It didn't stop him from explaining that his brother had an eye for beauty, and he even gestured at the pictures on the wall. The man would spend hours watching their guests, as Scott called them, without them even knowing it. In the darkness, they wouldn't be able to see the camera, just hear the click, click of the shutter as it closed, but the sound only added to their fear. The expensive infra-green camera with the night vision setting gave Scott and his brother a peek into the deepest caverns of those women's souls.

Scott's gaze slid up to stare at the pictures. I guessed he was having a little moment reminiscing about his homicidal brother. His voice softened as he kept his eyes locked on a certain spot behind me. I didn't attempt to catch a glimpse of what he was staring at. The only thing I wanted to focus on was you and how I would get you out of here because this couldn't be the end. I tried so hard to keep my mind focused on you, but Scott's brotherly tale kept forcing its way into my head.

I didn't care about how Travis had taught him to seek out the harsh realities that life had dealt him, to embrace the images of torture and bodies burned to a crisp, images brought on by a war that hadn't been his own. I didn't care about any of that, nor that he taught Scott to see those images for the art they were supposed to represent. *The art of life's end.*

It all sounded like some form of dictation, and when he handed me a stack of papers I wondered if he wanted me to write his memoir or something. Soon enough it became clear to me that he wanted your story. As if his brother's death had unleashed his own psychopathic creative tendencies.

At first, I hadn't mind as long as it kept him off my back. I gave him a shallow account of what had brought us here, but that wasn't what he wanted. I didn't know why, but he kept pushing and pushing, wanting more details—all about you. I had refused and only started to fill these stupid pages and revealing some of your story after I saw what he'd threatened to do to you. Somehow, it hadn't registered in my mind that he could have been hurting you ever since he had taken you. I had known it, but I didn't know what it meant.

After spending these past few days under the will of this psycho…you'd probably think that I shouldn't call him that, because he'll read everything I'll put down on the page. Perhaps, I shouldn't insult him, but that would mean I would be writing for him, and although I knew this to be true, my heart wrote these words for you. Deep down inside, a small sliver of hope still existed that we might get out of here and, more importantly, that you might get out of here. And perhaps then these words could reach you.

Just when I thought my mind was ready to form some string of profound words, Scott pulled me out of my haze. I tried to recapture them but wasn't able to hang on as he said, "Do you know how she did it? How she kept herself from losing her mind?"

My head had lolled down to my chest, and I had to strain myself to glance up at him. Your strength had always fascinated me. It turned out to be a fascinating thing to many people, and I wished it hadn't attracted the attention of Scott, but I was grateful at being introduced to it myself.

"I wouldn't have even noticed it if I hadn't spotted her from your place with a pair of binoculars, Matt," he said gleefully. "I'd barely caught her movement behind that tiny hole. She had kept her sanity because of the access to light and the world outside. That's why it had taken so much longer with her than with the others."

My heart sunk as I thought of you peeking through that hole, holding on to a tiny shred of life. *Holding on for what? For me?* In a way, I might have hoped you had been holding on for me, but considering how that turned out, I could only pray it wasn't the only thing that kept you going.

Scott added, "Could you have imagined

that? I hadn't seen it coming. I would never have thought her to be that bold, to defy me the way she had—at least not until you told me that story about her dad."

The sound of fascination in his voice urged me to look up. Facing the gleam in his eyes, I felt my blood run cold. As if he sensed that he had captured my attention, he nodded his head slowly and a smirk formed on his face.

He said, "Don't forget it was you who enlightened me about how I had misjudged her, regardless of how reluctant you were to share the information."

His words added to the guilt I already felt about revealing your secrets in the pages that had come before these. The look in his eyes added to the fear of what he might do to you. I had done it to protect you. The sight of him threatening you with a knife had made the decision easy, but I feared this wouldn't pan out the way I had hoped. *Perhaps I should have lied?* But Scott knew me too well; he would have known.

It was hard to ignore him after that, but

I wouldn't bother you with those details. I might have said it before, but I think this story is ending. Let's face it: all the roads leading up to here have crossed along the way, and it won't be long until the strings that keep Scott together will snap. I'm not for long good-byes and besides, my paper for today is spent.

I love you, Julie,
    Always.

Chapter Twenty-Five

Julie

Why did you have to come? I had almost started to believe that we would make it out of here, that you had rescued me from this place. Still, there wasn't room for blame inside my heart. *How could you have known your best friend had betrayed you?* That he couldn't feel contented anymore by preying on strangers? That he would do anything to quench his desires, even by destroying the lives of the ones he knew?

It was only when I heard his deep voice thundering across that yard after I saw him standing in that door opening that I realized who had kept me all this time, and somehow the pieces started to fall into place.

I remembered meeting him at your parent's party. He seemed so genially interested in me after he had learned I belonged to you. Of course, I shut down after the first few questions, remaining polite but replying with short, clipped responses. I never enjoyed conversing with strangers on my own for the first time, but your dad had kept you busy talking to some of his friends. Those men in suits and ties came across as even more intimidating, so I kept to my corner of the room and talked to him. He didn't seem to mind my evasive answers. He actually seemed to enjoy himself, to explore, how far he could go—how far I would let him. He didn't get very far. With his broad shoulders, he was too much of a man for me. He seemed too confident, too impressed with himself, and he had no idea he came across as a cocky son of a bitch. I felt intimidated by the way he loomed over me and tried to talk near my ear as if we were at a loud rock concert or something. I hadn't expected him to be so bold in his pursuit of what he wanted. Especially not inside your parents' home and with you there, but then I hadn't expected him to kidnap me.

When he realized he had reached his limit with me, he turned to your parents' art collection. He seemed to know what he was talking about as he pointed out areas on several canvasses, but then he could have been talking out of his ass. I didn't know anything about art. Working the night shift as a desk clerk at a clinic to put myself through school didn't leave much room for admiring art. It was you who introduced me to its beauty, but that's all that it would ever become—admiring a beautiful picture without understanding what meaning lay behind it. This had been enough for you, but he seemed eager to make me understand the depths that lay underneath the paintings.

That night I didn't pick up on the subtle remarks he made about how it was all about the story behind the picture, and if we didn't dig deep, we'd never be able to understand it. I just kept hoping you'd come to my rescue. He led me across the room and into your parent's library with the intent of showing me something. Nervously, I glanced around the room filled with large bookcases and noticed we were alone. Your father had been a vivid compiler of books about arts through the ages and had managed to obtain quite a collection.

Scott weaved around the classic wooden

furniture engraved with the most delicate carvings as if he owned the place. I waited, hovering near the door, feeling a long way away from my comfort zone. I had only met your parents a few times by then and didn't feel comfortable enough to stroll around their house on my own.

He, however, didn't seem to have a problem with it as he grabbed a book from one of the cases and flipped through the pages. With a pride-filled smirk on his face, he trotted back to me and lifted the book for me to see.

I glanced at it for a moment and then at him, unable to understand the admiring gleam in his eyes before I returned my attention to the rudimentary drawing. Broad strokes of what looked like charcoal depicted a woman strung up by her upper arms. One of her legs had been tied to the same rope and pulled up all the way behind her back so her foot nearly touched her head. Below the dangling figure, several faces peered up with interest at the horrific display.

He asked, "What do you see?"

I looked at him in disbelief and said, "This is what you wanted me to look at?" Without waiting for a reply, I turned on my heels, feeling eager to find you and go home. Behind me, he said, "You see the pain and the torture, don't you?"

"Is there anything else to see?" I said as I stopped at the door and turned to face him.

He said, "But you don't know the story behind it."

"I have no interest in knowing the story behind that picture," I said and stomped out of the room to find you. Maybe I should have stayed and listen. Maybe then all of this would have made more sense.

Chapter Twenty-Six

Julie

The words formed on their own accord as I scribbled them down on paper. The deceptions of thoughts rendered by my senses poured out of me, ready for him to read. He would read them every day after I'd placed my pen on the table, and he'd usher me away to my private hell inside that bathroom. *How often had he done that—four, five times?* This meant it had to be close to five days since you'd come for me, but only if I could actually translate the times he sat me in the chair into days. In the end, it wouldn't matter.

I didn't know whether he'd wait for you to finish yours or whether he read them while you were sitting in that chair.

I knew you had resisted him. I could tell from the way he'd slam the doors out of frustration. He'd never done that before. He hurt you, because that's what he did when he didn't get his way, but I never heard your screams. *Were you trying to be brave for me?* I wished I could be that brave. I wished I hadn't cried in the way I had when he came to get me from my room and forced me down on my knees in front of you.

The sight of you strapped in that chair nearly killed me. Your bloodied face looked swollen and bruised. You could barely see through the one eye that actually opened. He used me to get you to cooperate. It hadn't taken much of an effort on his part. The knife he had threatened to cut my eye with had sliced into my cheek, and his chokehold had left bruises on my neck. You had caved in an instant and picked up the pen.

You hadn't said anything, and the bruising kept me from reading your face. Your one good eye leaked a tear down your cheek, and I feared it might be resignation. *Had you given up?* I couldn't blame you—the thought had occurred to me numerous times—but somehow, imagining it resonating in your head angered me. I couldn't care less about my life, never much did.

It was my father who had told me early

on that I wasn't worth the food he'd placed on the table. Not that my father had ever worked a day in his life to put food on the table. It had been my mom who had taken care of me and told me not to listen to him. It had been *she* who had made me nurture that tiny flicker of hope that I could provide for a better life for her if only I could render her free from the monster she had married —and I had. I wished I could do the same for you.

I couldn't imagine anything else but that you would get to read these words. If I stopped imagining that, I might as well have killed myself. So after you do, I'd need you to do something for me. There are things about me that you never knew. Things that were too painful to talk about even to you, and even as this ink latched onto the page, I couldn't bring myself to put those words down. He would probably make sure that these words would come to haunt me, but with each day that passed, I cared less. Besides, this was meant for you.

Find my mom! *Find your mom?* I could

imagine you thinking those words. Yeah, and this wouldn't be the worst you'll come to find out about me. If anyone could explain what happened, it would be her. She understood my reasons, and I could only hope you would too one day.

I'd never intended to insinuate my mom had passed, but once conceived in your family's and your minds, it all had seemed it was meant to be. She'd known what I had done, and although I'd known she'd never tell a soul, it had scared me. It had scared me every time I'd looked at you, and the thoughts had crept into my mind. *What would you think of me when you found out?* I hadn't been able to bear those thoughts and chose to bury the life I once had. Besides, I had freed her from that bastard. She had been able to live the life she had always wanted.

I had never fully grasped the concept of love. It had seemed something that only existed in the movies and not meant for me until I met you. When my life had come to a halt, with the voices inside my mind the only place of being and sitting behind the glass my only comfort, I had come to understand love and especially the loss of it.

I had never realized I might have added to my mom's pain by shutting her out of my life. I had given her freedom but had also taken her daughter from her. *Was it too late to make things right?*

Watching you sit in that chair, all I wanted to do was for us to get out of here, and for some unintelligible reason, the thought of introducing you to my mom seemed important. I wanted to make things right for her and for you. If only I could do for you what I had done for her. If only I could set you free.

Chapter Twenty-Seven

Julie

Your I-supposed-former-friend Scott sprang a surprise on me today as he came for me. He even switched on the light and waited for my eyes to adjust so he could see my reaction, or maybe he wanted me to see his. It didn't stop my blood from running cold as he said, "I want you to tell me the story about your daddy today."

Those words ripped the air from my lungs, and I couldn't breathe. *How could he have known? Unless…you had told him.*

He basically had to drag me to the chair after that. On the table, he had stacked more sheets of paper than usual, which told me he expected a lengthy tale. None of that mattered anymore, because he had found out. If Scott hadn't found out from you, then chances were good that he had told you by now. Both options meant that I hadn't been the one to tell you my secret. Endless scenarios of how you might have reacted to my deception crowded my mind. *Would you ever be able to forgive me?* The knowledge that you had found out my darkest secret had changed something inside me, and on that sixth or seventh day after you had joined me, I had made my decision.

As he watched me from a distance, sitting in a corner on the floor, he couldn't know what raged through my mind. I hadn't looked up at him, but I knew he had that gleeful smirk on his face. I hadn't even looked up from this sheet of paper. It wasn't that I couldn't face him. The hate he stirred inside me would make it easy to face him, but it wasn't him that kept my eyes down.

I had seen his wall of trophies before and even though he had told me they were his brother's work, I could read the pride from his eyes as he spoke of them.

One picture after another hung in a perfect order where they got more gruesome as they progressed. All these people, all those lives destroyed by the insanity of these two men. I couldn't look at them because I knew he would relish in the fact, and I wouldn't give him that. I was also afraid I might find one of you and feared it would bring him even more joy. So I kept my eyes on the page.

An involuntary twitch rattled my body as he started to speak. His words were soft as he tried to coax my mind. I sensed his sincerity and it threw me aback. His words didn't come as a surprise. I had thought of them myself many times. He wanted me to embrace my past.

I wondered if he thought that he knew me after finding out what I had done, and perhaps he did. Maybe he had guessed it from the story he had been told. He had watched me long enough these past months and might even know me better than I knew myself. So it wouldn't come as a surprise to him as he read my confession on this page. By now he had to have figured out that this creature he had kept in his cage all this time wasn't some docile pet he could control. He must have realized that, for once, he had found a kindred spirit that lived by rules similar to his, because I had killed someone.

It felt strange writing these words on this

page. If you hadn't yet, then I never intended for you to find out this way, but he had left me no choice. I should have probably apologized beforehand, but it wasn't as if I were a storyteller. Still, it pained me that I had never told you the truth, and I hoped you would forgive me. There wasn't enough paper in the world that could hold the words of how I felt about you. I hoped you knew that.

For what I had done, I knew I wouldn't be able to form the words in an order that might absolve me so here they come in the form of the cold, hard truth: *I have killed my father with every intention of killing him.*

I wouldn't delve into the reasons, because there wouldn't be enough paper in the world, except for the fact that I hated him. I hated him for what he had done to my mom and what he had put her through all those years, and I hated him for what he had done to me.

So now both of you know what I had done. *Did it matter?* Probably not. I did what I did to survive, and you could think of me what you wanted, because I would do it again. Down to the basics, we were all animals programmed to survive no matter what the cost, and my instincts were strong. It didn't matter who got hurt in the process. You did what you did to survive.

My cards had been dealt, my secrets spilled, and I have come to the end of my page. The thought that you might never look at me as you once did, hurts in ways I wouldn't be able to describe, but that was okay—I am finished. I refuse to spend another day like this. I need to know that I am ready, and now that I see the gleam in his eyes as he watches me accept the horrors he had caused, I know I am. I am ready now, and I apologize, my love, but I have to do this. As his words become louder, I realize he had been right about one thing. I had been kidding myself these past few years thinking I could leave behind the person I once was. I wouldn't be able to live with myself if I didn't try to embrace my true self, and this was the only way I could think of, so please, Matthew, stop reading.

Scott,

This is what you wanted, wasn't it? You wanted to strip my soul and lay it bare, well here you have it. You have revealed my secrets and found the truth that lies underneath the surface. I hope you're pleased with yourself, because you have unleashed the darkness I have tried to keep at bay. I am willing to give this to you as long as you let Matthew go. It's all yours—I'm yours.

Chapter Twenty-Eight

Scott

I've been sitting in the corner, watching Julie work for a while. It seemed impossible for me to take my eyes off her, although the hard wooden floor was starting to do a number on my back. My muscles ached, but watching her made it worth it. Although the lighting was dim, her pale skin seemed to glow in the gloom. She had lost a considerable amount of weight in the time she had been in here, but it accentuated her sharp features and, in my eyes, made her more beautiful than I had ever seen her.

She sat with her back straight and her eyes down as her hand danced across the page. I could watch her work like that forever.

"Do you even know what I'm trying to do here," I said. Julie flinched at the sound of my voice but otherwise remained undeterred. It seemed I was in for a one-sided conversation. "I know you don't want to face it—just as you didn't want to face the story behind that picture I once showed you."

It had been her reaction to that picture that made me notice it. Up until that point, she had been polite and patient with me even though I could tell she hadn't been comfortable the entire time. The moment I confronted her with the violent image on the page, she had shut me down and fled the room. Her reaction had intrigued me and was part of the reason I had recommended her to Travis. I hadn't told him she'd been my buddy's fiancée. That had been a mistake on my part. Not the fact that I knew her, but the fact that I had recommended her.

"You should embrace your story," I added, "not shy away from it."

Her eyes remained focused on the page as if her life depended on it and in her mind it probably did. She couldn't know that I wanted more for her. She had held on for so long. I didn't think I had ever seen a person endure in the way she had. The more I watched Travis work around her taking his pictures and failing to grasp her mental decline, the more she drew me in.

Unfortunately, she had a similar effect on Travis except he wanted her to break. It was Travis who wanted to involve Matthew, especially after he had found his way across the street. Travis thought it would solve two problems at the same time. He would be able to use Matthew to break Julie's armor so he would finally have his pictures and simultaneously rid himself of a person pointing fingers at him.

"You have to know," I said to Julie, "that Matthew will never be able to see past what you truly are—not anymore."

I watched her for a moment to gauge her reaction. It seemed to make her scribble her pen across the page with more determination, and I got to my feet.

I wasn't able to reason with Travis that going after Matthew might shift a lot more focus his way. It hadn't been a passionate argument—Travis would do whatever he would do, and I would support him in that. Except for the first time in my life, I felt the urge to disagree with him. I wanted Travis to have his picture—for him to fill that need he so desperately wanted, but I also wanted something else—I wanted Julie. It seemed Matthew had removed my doubt from the equation by killing Travis. He would pay for that, but with it, he had given me Julie.

It wouldn't be long before the police would appear. Matthew had made enough ruckus and pointed as many fingers at my brother that, of course, the law would stop by soon enough. Perhaps not with the intention to charge anyone, but surely to ask questions and with Travis dead that might become problematic. Besides, I'd never be able to rid myself of the evidence left inside this house, and I wasn't about to dig up the bodies Travis had me bury down in that basement in the first place. The house had belonged to Travis, and he was dead. But just in case, I had called Matthew's mother and reassured her that he was fine. She'd sounded worried and wanted to talk to him, but I had convinced that we'd been out on a binge. She didn't sound too happy that I was trying to help Matthew to drown Julie's memory in alcohol, but I guessed I had bought myself a few days.

Now I had to figure out what to do with these two. Matthew wasn't the problem. Though he had been my surrogate brother when we were kids, I didn't think I'd have any trouble slicing his throat—not after what he had done to Travis. *But Julie…Julie, Julie, what to do with her?* I knew what I wanted from her, but I didn't know if she'd be ready for what I had to offer—I wanted her to come with me.

I stepped closer to the table as she filled the page with certain urgency. I couldn't wait to read it, but that wasn't the reason why I wanted her to write her story. Putting words on a page made the truth come to life just as Travis had done with his pictures. The written word, as with the image, gave it texture. It might help Julie to find herself.

Matthew's words had caused a revelation. They had shed a light on all the secrets Julie had kept from me, and along with that hole in the foil, it might have been the true reason for why she had kept it together. Something changes you after you have taken a life, something fundamental, which makes you stronger and more resilient than the rest. It feeds you, and now the truth about how Julie had experienced this would come out.

Julie had kept shying away from that truth, instead of embracing it. That's why I had to give her a little incentive. To coax out her true self and by doing that, she might even be able to save herself. I wanted to see it blossom.

"Do you even understand what I'm doing for you," I said. Her uncaring posture lit a fire inside my chest, demanding a reaction. "Do you think building up this fake existence with Matt has done you any good? He made you forget who you truly are—I'm trying to set you free here." My voice got louder as I spoke those last words. I wasn't deliberately looking for a fight with Julie, but I needed to find that trigger that would set her free. We had more in common than she would ever dare to admit, and I wanted to see it.

Standing next to the table, I crossed my arms and stood as I had done so many times before as I entered the room while she cowered in that bathtub. She wasn't cowering anymore. In fact, she hadn't cowered since I had brought her up the stairs and locked her inside that bathroom after I'd stopped Matthew from taking her from me. Travis had been right. Matthew had been the trigger, but I didn't think it had been the one that Travis would have had in mind.

"All it needed was removing some clothes from your house, and creating the right atmosphere among Matt's friends and even with the police," I said. "Nobody cared that you were gone, a piece of white trash, a dead dad, and a trailer park mom. Who would care about that? It just needed the right incentive." I paused for a moment, waiting for a retort, but it didn't come. If I wanted her to join me, she would have to part with her old life, and although I knew that wouldn't be easy, I had to start somewhere.

"There is something wrong with that girl."

"Can't you tell from the way she never seems to make eye contact?"

"She avoids talking to any of Matt's friends— haven't you noticed?"

"Have you ever talked to her, I mean really?"

I said every line with a deliberate pause, but Julie didn't take the bait.

As if she hadn't heard a single word that had come from my mouth, Julie kept her pen moving across the page.

"It wasn't hard to spread the seed of doubt in the minds of Matt's friends," I said. "Even Matthew, I basically had to drag him over here to convince him that you were here." I paused, searching for a reaction, but it didn't come, and I decided to change tactic. "I guessed it didn't help that they found out you killed your daddy."

For the briefest of moments, her head twitched, and then the pen stopped moving. A smile grew on my face. *I had her.*

I watched Julie sitting in an immaculate

pose with her back straight, hands folded in her lap, and eyes on the paper.

This morning I hadn't bothered with restraining her to the chair. Her body had hung limp as I carried her from the bathroom, and I feared I might break her like a twig. It didn't seem worth the effort to tie her up. Somewhere between then and lifting the pen from the page, she had composed herself.

I narrowed my eyes to watch her. She sat as still as a wax statue as if she were waiting for me. She couldn't have finished writing. I had told her that I wanted the story of her deepest and darkest secret with every gruesome detail of how she had killed her daddy and how it had made her feel. She didn't look like someone who just spilled her worst moment. She seemed too calm. *Was she contemplating how I had found out? Was she worried Matthew might have found out?*

From where I stood, she appeared so fragile, and it seemed impossible for her to have retained her sanity. But from up close, it wasn't hard to miss that something darker sat hidden behind those eyes, something that must have helped her to survive. For anyone else, the solitude alone would have been torturous to the mind, even with that small connection to the outside world.

I stepped in front of the sliver of light coming from the light bulb hanging from the ceiling. It's amazing how the right type of bulb could affect a room's atmosphere.

My shadow loomed over her, but Julie didn't move. She didn't even flinch. This didn't come close to the Julie that always seemed to fidget with something, whether it was the fabric of her clothes or biting her nonexistent nails.

The wood cracked underneath my boots as I rounded the table, but still she didn't move. For a second I thought she might have stopped breathing, but then I saw her chest move. It rose and fell in a slow and controlled rhythm.

I changed my own breathing pattern to a slow, heavy rhythm, which always seemed to tick her off, but still she didn't move. My shadow engulfed the table as I moved around and stopped behind her. I leaned in, placing my hands on the table, and trapped her between my arms. I lowered my head and caressed my lips along her left ear before I whispered into it.

"You can't expect me to believe you've finished," I said in a low voice. Julie maintained her nonresponsive act, and I decided to up my game.

"Can you?" I bellowed into her ear. Finally, I managed to get her to react. She jumped at the sound of my voice but composed herself immediately after. Something had changed, and I wondered what had brought it on. My eyes flickered to the scribbles on the page, and I gathered it up as I kneeled at her side.

"What have you made for me?" I asked. As I scanned the page, I noticed her head shifted a tiny bit. She watched me as I read. It set off a jolt of anticipation, figuring she'd experienced the same emotion while she waited for my reaction. I couldn't imagine that these meager words could hold the secrets I was hoping for, but still, I yearned for some insight into her soul. I glanced at her from the corner of my eye, but couldn't really make the connection of this tender looking female and the fact she had murdered her father. I felt the urge to know more to find out everything I could about this tainted life. If I were honest with myself, I doubted if I would ever be able to part with her. I wanted her, unlike anything I had ever wanted in my life.

The thought hadn't even left my mind as my elation drained, reading her first words on the page. Her story was nothing more than a speech directed at Matthew. I glanced up at her, wondering what she was playing at, but her eyes shifted to the tabletop, like some subservient animal, and I read on.

Her apologetic tone of voice on the page seemed to change, and it stirred something inside me. As if her fears of what Matthew might have thought of her slowly seeped from her mind as the reality of what she had done took center stage. She had seemed adamant to convey that her words were directed at Matthew, but somehow I could read it between the lines. Behind this creature so frail and tender on the surface hid a predator, bent on survival.

With every word I read, I witnessed the truth between the lines. *She was more like me than I could have imagined.* I still felt the loss of Travis, but the words on this page eased the pain. The knowledge that without Travis, Julie could be mine eased that pain and now it seemed as if she herself had opened the door for that to happen.

She hadn't done what I had asked. These words held no details of what had happened between her and her father, but I couldn't help feeling pleased. At least she had finally confessed to what had happened without any apologies and with that had made the first step to reaching her full potential. I felt a connection to her that I had never felt with anyone and wondered if the fight would even leave her eyes just before she blew out her last breath, but I wasn't planning to find out.

The delightful feeling soon left as she

directed her words back to Matthew. Anger started to rise inside me as I came upon those final sentences. Everything always seemed to revolve around him. I didn't understand what she saw in him. He had always been weak. He would never have been able to bring himself to see Julie for who she truly was. Perhaps I should get rid of him now and observe how she would deal with it. I frowned at her apologetic words to Matthew and I glanced up at her, but she wouldn't meet my eyes. *Ready for what?*

My eyes returned to the page feeling a combination of surprise and disappointment. I looked up after I read her final words. *Did these words reveal the truth? Had she finally surrendered to me?* Her head shifted, and her eyes locked with mine. She stared at me, with eyes filled with hate. Somehow, it turned me on to see her looking at me like that. As if all my efforts of trying to set her free her had come to this, her final moment of defiance before she could embrace her own being. I stared at her and felt my heart weaken in her presence. She would have become my brother's greatest piece even though *he* wouldn't have been able to add to her shine—no one could add to her perfection.

My lips curved into a smile. I couldn't help it. Julie's gaze, however, turned as dark as I had ever seen it before she opened her mouth to speak. Her words weren't what I expected.

"Die, you motherfucker!" Julie screamed in my face. I barely caught the momentum of her arm with my eyes, but I felt the pain as she slammed her fist into my neck. It took me a moment to register. The sensation of pain I felt didn't compute with the sight of this weakened young woman. Then it hit me as my eyes flickered over the tabletop. The pen Julie had used to write her words was gone.

Accompanied by another scream from Julie, a second sharp pain dug into my neck. As I felt the warm, slick blood trail down my collarbone, it finally sank in what she had done, and I shoved her. She fell backward along with the chair and landed with a thud on the ground. I used the table to pull myself to my feet. The anger building inside me morphed into rage. My hands balled into fists, ready to release my rage on Julie's pretty face, but my legs wouldn't comply. Strength rushed from my body like water down a drain. My heart hammered inside my chest, but instead of fueling my rage, I could feel my determination waver along with my legs.

As my hand grasped for my neck in an attempt to plug the hole that seems to be depleting my strength, the chair scraped along the floor, and I turned to the sound. Julie screamed like a lunatic as she lifted it off the ground. I faced her just in time to deflect the blow with my arm, but one of my legs buckled. I fell to the ground to one knee and looked up to see Julie's face contorted in an animalistic growl as she lifted the chair again.

My eyes remained locked on hers. I couldn't turn away. Nothing remained of the fragile little woman that I had come to know. The expression on her face told me everything I needed to know. It hid nothing of the story I wanted from her. A feeling of pride filled me inside along with the loss of what could have been if she only had chosen to be mine.

The chair swooshed through the air and connected hard with my face. I fell backward, and my head hit the wooden floor. As I lay there on my back, I could hear the blood rush through my veins along with the faint beating of my heart.

Through the open door, I heard the footsteps of bare feet slapping on the floor.

My mind raced, raking through my memories of this woman who had seemed so fragile yet, at the same time, so strong. I had watched her for so long, seen the despair in her eyes as everything seemed lost and witnessed how she balanced precariously on the edge of insanity. Her words on the page seemed so sincere. *How could I have misinterpreted them?* She was supposed to reclaim herself and embrace the gifts I had given her.

A door clicked in the distance, and I

heard Julie's muffled cries. Shocked rippled through me as I recognized Matthew's voice, and he called out her name. *No, no, no,* I wanted to shout, but nothing more than a nasty gurgling sound exited my throat. *This couldn't be. This wasn't how this story was supposed to end. How could she have deceived me with a mind so far gone? There had to be truth to her words on the page.*

I listened to their footfalls along with the cracks of the wooden steps as I lay there waiting for the rush in my veins to still and the beating of my heart to fade. *Even I had underestimated her?* This final thought lingered in my mind as I heard the faint sound of a lock clicking. As my vision turned dark, the front door creaked open and then slammed shut.

Behind the Glass

M. Van

Thanks for picking up this book and I hope you've enjoyed it. I would really appreciate it if you left a review.

If you would like to find out more, visit www.42links.net and join the mailing list.

Other books
by
M. Van

The Wheels and Zombies series

Ash: A novella in the Wheels and
Zombies series

Brooklyn, Wheels and Zombies

Aground: Book Three in the Wheels and
Zombies series